# DIRT UPON
# MY SKIN

# Dirt Upon My Skin

by

## Steve Toase

BLACK SHUCK
SHADOWS

Black Shuck Books
www.BlackShuckBooks.co.uk

Versions of the following stories first appeared as follows:
'The Ercildoun Accord' in *Lackington's Magazine* #25 (2022)
'To Rectify in Silver' in *Nightmare Magazine* #111 (2021)
'God in a Box' in *Cafe Irreal* #36 (2010)
'Dirt Upon My Skin' in *Animal Day II* (Not One of Us, 2018)
'Traverse' in *In the Blink of an Eye* (Roxton Press, 2019)
'Tuppence a Bag' in *They're Out to Get You! Volume One: Animals and Insects* (TK Pulp, 2021)
'Horn and Hoof' in *Roar and Thunder* (2011)
'Terminus Post Quen' in *Mad Scientist Journal* (2019)

Cover design & internal layout © WHITEspace 2024
www.white-space.uk

First published in the UK by Black Shuck Books, 2024

978-1-917173-99-5

*For Trix*

*10YR 4/3*

*Be an archaeologist, they said.*

*See the world, they said.*

The
Ercildoun
Accord

*Small Finds Nos. 034-082*
*A series of small metal coins, heavily worn through apparent use. Each coin is stamped on the reverse and obverse. Larger than standard coinage and heavier, with a golden appearance. During the preparation to remove the finds from site, the material was identified as: leaves (variously sycamore, elm, and ash), sheep's wool, and bone dust.*

—*Extract from* Small Find Report
Excavations in the Lower Kingdom
of the Seven Silken Ghosts

~

I pour the hot fat into the concentric circles and watch it settle against the stone. The winds across the moor are fresh, cooling the fat white and opaque. In the central hammerstone-chipped cup I pour the whiskey, the alcohol staying golden. For years we did not know what the cup and ring stones were used for until we found the Calkerdale Stone in a peat bog, offerings preserved by the lack of air and death.

The irony of using prehistory as a gateway to study prehistory does not escape me. I place my hand against the rock, feeling the grain shift beneath my touch. The surface softens and flexes against my weight and then I'm reaching through for another place.

For a few moments after I arrive my skin is grey and glittered with feldspar, then fades back to normal flesh. In this place I feel myself ageing as everything around me does not. I can feel myself rotting with life.

Ignoring the sensation of decay I close my eyes and open them again to take in my surroundings. Above me the sun is always setting but never set. I breathe in the air of Faery and wonder if I will make it out this time or if something else will look out through my eyes. My hand goes to the hawthorn and linen thread hanging around my neck and I shudder despite myself.

The place where I've arrived is deserted. The agreement between the Choked Monarchs and our company does not allow me to approach the Royal Cities. Instead I am required to travel directly to the excavation site.

I look back toward the stone that stands behind me, but it has dissolved like sugar in rain, leaving bones in the grass hollow. I wipe a smear of grease from my hands. My fingers smell of peat, though whether from the single malt or the bog from where I travelled I do not know.

We all have our ways of dealing with the journey into the Deathless Kingdom. I open my hipflask and take a sip as my way of coping.

I set up the tent, canvas soaked in oils for protection. As I unpack the flysheets and poles the area fills with the scent of cat urine and mould-spotted bread. Not for the first time I wish that some of the ancient folk stories were not true.

All my equipment is old. Plane tables and alidades. Vintage transit levels encased in sturdy varnished timber boxes. Wood and brass. No iron or electrics. That lesson was learnt by the first archaeologists who made the journey across, their bones welded to their surveying devices by Faery's allergy to iron.

After my shelter is ready, my next job is to mark out the trench for excavation. I don't have many hours until my presence is noted, either by the stench of my mortality on the wind or the gossip of the Faery Court. I want to be set up before a delegation arrives so that I will not be distracted when forced to indulge in the tedious riddles that seem necessary for every interaction with the inhabitants of this twisted land.

Using wooden stakes I mark out a trench twenty metres long and two metres wide. Only once during the setting out do the ropes transform into adders. I look around for the source but cannot see any puckas or redcaps lurking at the treeline. Reminding myself the serpents are just a glamour I drive blackthorns into the snakes' tails, watching the ropes shrug off their deceit. I continue with the measurements to make sure that the trench is straight.

The Thing of Blemished Claws is the first to visit the excavation, face decorated in tendons from a recent meal. I am still organising the paperwork and I pay no attention to its approach. In the distance I hear other inhabitants, their steps only audible because they make that choice. I do not see them and focus on finishing my preparations.

~

*In Faery, the Land is the Monarch and the Monarch is the Land. In Faery, there is no metaphor. Any division between the two is a delusion. When excavating in any of the kingdoms, as much care should be taken as if you were performing surgery. Appropriate offerings should be placed around the edge of the trench to anaesthetise the ground. Each spade cut is a scalpel blade going into the Monarch's flesh. Each bucketful of soil carried away is a scar left on the Regal Torso. You will attract attention. You will be tested. You will have to account for yourself.*

—Dr Gwen Sedbusk, Guidelines for
Archaeological Excavations
in Otherworld Locations

~

The pyres of valerian and willow bark send up smoke plumes that hang in the air. There is no breeze to disperse them and they accumulate around me as I begin to strip back the turf, laying the grass-heavy tiles to one side. Beyond the fumes The Burning Children eat a picnic of toasted fear and boiled sorrow. They only observe me and do not attempt to interfere.

Directly below the root mat the subsoil is butterfly wings, fluttering as the overburden is lifted. I plan the layers, then shovel them away to get to the focus of my work, trying to ignore the spoilheap's attempts to take flight. The graves are clear in the natural, not that anything in this place is natural.

~

There is no history in Faery. Not really. History would imply some kind of written record. The Faery Court can barely agree on what colour the sky is, never mind reach a consensus on the past. For our records we class the prehistory of Faery as anything before Robert Kirk wrote his treatise on the place. It makes no difference. Time is fickle here. Everything is eternal and fleeting.

I begin to plan the features. Cutting across the site is a single ditch, backfilled with precious stones. Opals, rubies and sapphires glitter in the ground, worthless in their abundance. I shovel them out of the way, drawing the plan and section, taking a sample of the fill, knowing it, in time, will turn to seeds or dust.

The ditch cuts three of the graves but several darken the bottom of the trench without any later disturbance. As I walk around the trench I avoid stepping on the grave fills. In the soil the shadows of those interred twitch and convulse. If I concentrate I can hear their voices turned hoarse by the dirt.

I decide to leave them in the ground one more day.

I do not sleep, the sound of the Faery Rade processing around the excavation disturbing my rest. I do not bother to look out. No one will be there. In the morning my tent is stitched up with nettle thread. It takes me several hours to cut my way out. Every time I sever the cord it whips back together.

Once I have countered the prank I sit outside and eat my breakfast. The Herald approaches as I finish, its still-living pennant stretched by roughly pierced brass eyelets, its screams and sobbing too loud in the silent landscape.

"I bring greetings from the Choked Monarchs of the Coruscate Palace, the Three Siblings of the Honeysuckle Matricide, the Victors of the Festering Wood. They compliment you on your scent and wish you moderate success in your pointless endeavours."

I take a breath and put my cup to one side. "Please send my greetings in return, and my thanks for allowing us to undertake this important work to help foster better links between our two worlds."

The Herald laughs and the pennant squeals in agony.

"They have no interest in any diplomacy between our worlds. They are only interested in the mild diversion of your presence. With luck you might become mortally wounded during your work so that they can suspend you at the moment of death and enjoy your perishment."

"Will you thank their Majesties for their consideration? Of course, if I feel myself on the verge of expiring, I will call on the servants of the Court to preserve the moment in perpetuity for the delight of the occupants of the Charred Thrones."

"Our skin-flayers and embalmers are at your disposal."

With a deep bow the herald strides back across the meadow, kicking divots through the air with its pierced feet.

Once I am sure the Herald has left the area I remove all the food it has concealed in my supplies, watching it turn to spores as I throw it to the dirt.

~

*The second article of the Ercildoun Accord between the Nation States of the Waking World and the Choked Monarchs of the Lesser Tenebrous Court allows one (1) representative of Multi-vallate Archaeology to enter the profane territories and carry out targeted excavation in the Fields of the Tarnished Orchestra. The aim of the excavation is to allow for the recovery of remains lost in the territories of the Court during the recognised Prehistoric Period of that land (∞-present), for the purpose of recovering human remains (number unspecified). The archaeologist may only excavate human remains predating first official recognised contact between the Waking World and the Perpetual Realms. Any deviation will be seen as a disparagement of the diplomatic relations between our worlds and treated accordingly.*

—Article 2, Ercildoun Accord

~

The first grave is child-sized and I begin to chase the edge, scraping the fill back from the natural until the cut is clear and precise. From below the soil voices continue to taunt me. I consider plugging my ears against the tricks, but in this place I need all my senses, as fragile as they are.

Before I break for food I reveal the first bones. They are narrow and corroded and for a moment I picture the chains of ancestry that led to the birth of this one person. I see their parents catching each other's gaze across a bar, or passing a word in the noise of a nightclub. I picture the scuffed bedclothes and the crib, and I feel the loss and grief like a cloud of ash.

Taking a break, I walk through the meadow to clear my head. The vegetable lambs mew as I brush against them, snapping at my clothes in their disturbance.

When I return to the trench the loose has been returned to the grave and I spend the next hour returning to my first point of progress.

The bones are the colour of peat water, stained and accreted by time, but still recognisable in the stillness of death. With care I lift the soil from the skeleton, the bones fused where they should not be and articulated where no joint should occur. Yet despite the appearance, the glamour imposed on the remains, I know this person came from the same place as me. Would have walked the same streets, if they had not been cradle-snatched. If they had not been prised from their nursery. From their parents. I wonder if there is a body in a grave somewhere back in the waking world where the bones are returned to sticks as the glamour erodes. In the ground the remains whimper as if they have not been told they are dead. They smell of wet cardboard and sour cream. I clean the ribs off best I can and prepare to lift them.

~

In their plastic bags the bones look slight and diminished. What they represent, the humanity and the loss, is lessened by the process of my profession, but in this place, where the world changes on a whim, my procedures anchor me.

I sense the scrutiny of the Faery Court as I continue recording, labelling and bagging the remains. Beside the body I find several artefacts: a baby's rattle, a single golden coin, the remains of a soil-stained blanket. Until I return I have no way of knowing if they are genuine or legerdemain. I treat them as authentic and record them.

The Travelling Court arrives as I start work on the second burial. I only sense their presence by the scent of saltwater on the air and a shimmer of verdigris in the corner of my eye. After two hours they reveal themselves.

Two hundred and twenty-two creatures crowd the trench edge, all trying to observe the uncovering of the burial. I ignore them. Not interacting is the best way to not transgress and transgression is sport to the Choked Monarchs. When they communicate it is through the pucka, a creature of spit and branches that drives a flint knife into its mouth before speaking.

"How go your endeavours? The siblings are incredibly interested in your progress." Moths tip from between its lips and it pulls them apart one by one.

"Slow and considered," I say and continue with the excavation.

"And will you be remaining long?"

"As long as it takes to excavate all the remains and prepare them for travel."

The burial I am currently uncovering is also accompanied by grave-goods. I find two bronze knives, a small bracelet of gold and three glass beads. The pucka reaches down to grab one of the blades and I move it beyond reach. A grin splits the bark of its face wider, but the eldest of the Royal Siblings reaches out and digs razor nails into its scalp.

"We are not to interfere. We are not to disrupt your work. We do not agree with this situation. We have no choice. If we had, our conditions would have been far more punitive."

The sibling pauses.

"Maybe we would have insisted on your intestines being on the outside of your torso, or your lungs filled with poppy seeds. Your tasks are boring and we have no interest."

~

*The residents of Faery place no value on artefacts, beyond their novelty. This means that the diligent researcher can build up a complex picture of the intrigues and interests of the rival factions through the archaeological record. By treading a fine line of etiquette and determination, there are many opportunities to build up a detailed picture of these complex societies.*

—*Dr Gwen Sedbusk*, Guidelines for
Archaeological Excavations
in Otherworld Locations

~

They leave and when they have gone I take a moment to catch my breath. In the trench the remains climb out of the grave, disarticulate themselves, and I watch the separated arms crawl across the soil into the finds bag.

Tipping the bag out I wait until the pucka has reassembled itself before grabbing it by the scruff of the neck. It tries to struggle free from my grip. Emptying my pocket I take out the silver coin soaked in vinegar and press it into the creature's mouth. While I still hold tight, it folds in upon itself and scrawls scars on the air as it is returned to the Royal Court.

Once the trickster has left, the remains are still in the grave. Now I am alone I can see the bones have been shattered and gilded. There is no way of knowing if the gilding is real, but I treat it as such. First I plan the grave, drawing each splinter of bone in its place, before gently prising it away from the dirt.

This body is silent, yet in its own way it still speaks to me. I hear the first time it awoke in the Hall of Salted Faces and saw the Court stare down at it like the curiosity they considered it to be. I see the person they were, providing amusement for the Courtiers, until this land of artifice could no longer sustain them and they perished, the flesh stripped from their bones as a delicacy, their bones covered in rare metal as a novelty.

The invite arrives a few moments before my transportation. And I am caught in a Cornelian dilemma. Refuse and I offend the Monarchs. Accept and I break the conditions of the agreement for my presence in Faery. I read the notice again. It is written on the inside of a desiccated crow and it is hard to concentrate as the bird recites bad poetry. The carriage is decorated in spirals of lichen, marsh gas burning in place of any driver. There are no horses or oxen. The harness is snagged with grass and the pulped remains of still-bleating vegetable lambs. While I delay I prise several free. They show no gratitude and bite my fingers raw.

I know I cannot obstruct much longer so I place the bird back in the carriage and bow to the driver.

"Please thank their honours for their consideration. As they may be aware, I am unable to approach the Royal Court due to the conditions of the agreement between their House and my organisation. If they would like to inform me of another suitable location, I would be more than happy to attend on their whim."

I struggle to make out any expression but the features are hard to see through the flames. He leaves, driving the horseless carriage through the long grass and I return to my work.

The Court arrives during the night, erupting from the soil fully formed, stretching through the birth caul of the land. I am in the middle of the Throne Room, my trench below the tiled floor. Courtiers dance around me, their gowns covered in carvings and pressed gold sheets.

The walls of the hall are hidden behind cuckoo spit and wilting flowers. Several skin bags hang from hooks, their contents squirming in their containment. I do not look too closely.

The youngest sibling dismounts the dais, their vast hands obscured by clouds.

"You appear to be in the Throne Room, contrary to the agreement between your company and our Court. This tastes like..." They pause as slaked lime tumbles out of their mouth to scorch the Courtiers that surround them. They giggle in their agonies. "Yes, this tastes like transgression. A breaking of contract. You humans do like to transgress."

I look around me. I am surrounded by the Amaranthine Guard. Their weapons are held aloft, the chipped stone blades naked. I stand and stretch out my hands.

"If your Lordships wanted to trick me into breaking our compact, surely there are less extravagant ways to humiliate someone as insignificant to you as I."

The laughter sounds like thorns against skin.

"Of course we do not manifest our desires this way, because of your value. We do it for our entertainment."

Their hands grab me and they pin me to the ground. I can see all the human remains. All the catalogues abandoned. Forgotten. I wonder if others will come to find me.

First they strip me and tie a band of fox fur around my arm. They paint my skin with copper until I glisten in the lights of the Court. As the Guards prepare me the Courtiers crowd around like I am a new skit or ballad.

They feed me burnt bread stuffed with mistletoe. When I try to refuse, knowing the meal will anchor me to this land of lies, the pucka forces apart my jaw, then stitches my lips shut with embroidery thread. Then they kill me. First they walk across me, hoofs and talons breaking my ribs. They want me to sing. Want me to be their brazen bull, my agony exhaled for them. I refuse and stay silent. With my face to the ground, they loop sinew around my neck and tighten until I have no voice anymore, and then they shatter my skull, scooping out portions of what's within to share amongst the most honoured of the Court.

They leave me for three days and nights in the middle of the Throne Room as they indulge in their masquerades and intrigues. On the fourth day they strap me to a stretcher and drag me through the fields to the peat bog.

Between the reeds and sphagnum moss they drop me into the water and leave me for the land to preserve. For my bones to soften to paste and my skin to harden to leather. I do not know if they will return or even if they will remember I am in the water, never rotting, never dying. In their trap I have become archaeology. Lying below the surface of peat, waiting for time and dirt to compress me to soil.

# To Rectify in Silver

At least twice a day it occurs to Marissa that the photos she uses to find Neolithic long barrows and Roman forts were taken to better plot destruction. Every image passing through her hands is labeled at the top in a language she cannot speak. A freezing of the land to ease the locating of bombs and the advancing of invasions. What she prizes in the silver nitrate landscapes are incidental. At least twice a day Marissa catches herself and has to lean back from the stereoscope to clear her mind of the horrors of war. Shattered bone and the accidental dead.

She writes down coordinates for several intercutting hut circles, then moves one photo to the side, slides the second across, and places another one down.

When she first studied archaeology, Marissa imagined herself sitting in trenches on gently rolling chalk downs. Striding across earthworks staring down the barrel of a Total Station as she recorded the ebb and flow of prehistoric topography. Not stuck in a windowless room in the basement of a concrete block surrounded by stacks of old manila envelopes that smell of acacia gum and dust.

She catches sight of Simon's photo pinned up behind the desk, taken just before the accident, and shudders at the memory. Turns her attention back to the pile of work. The photos still left to study.

There is magic here, conjured when two aerial photographs are brought together under the twin lenses of the stereoscope. Landscapes resurrected.

She leans forward, her back feeling the strain of six months staring into the past, and slides the two photos until the images come together. One moment, there is a doppler of hills and streets, the next a three-dimensional monochrome landscape. She lets herself fall into the contours, watching hanging valleys and frozen waterfalls manifest. Tracing earthworks caught in strafing sunshine along the steep deserted fields.

She knows Daltondale and the surrounding moors as well as her own town, if not better. She knows the strip fields near the villages, marked in stone walls and memory. She knows the vast straight enclosure boundaries transferred from surveyor's map to the commons. And she knows the Daltondale Henge that stands in the middle of the upland moor, now overgrown and half forgotten, but in the photos clear and bare from heather burning.

The Henge is already recorded. Already well known. Her project is to find all those features now hidden by the undergrowth. No matter what she is searching for, she always returns to the vast banked enclosure, curving ditches on the inside filled with silt and weeds. The centre covered in a scatter of recumbent stone. At the end of each day, she allows a moment to spread out the two photos. Uses the feature to centre herself.

The banks are uneven. Bulbous and bisected, like two loops of distended muscle. It is her anchor. A reassurance of stability as she studies the changing land.

~

The two photos are still underneath the stereoscope when she arrives at work the next morning. While the kettle boils, steaming the grey pitted wall, Marissa rearranges the photos so they swim into three dimensions once more. She is a minor god shaping rock like wet clay.

She notices something isn't right straight away, but struggles to put her finger on what it is. Whether it is the lack of alignment in the photos, or a shadow cast from some object in her office.

She leans back, closes and opens her eyes, then looks again.

The prone stones in the centre of the henge have sunk. Not far, but noticeable. Around the edge of each one is a rim of bare peat, their upper, roughly hewn faces below ground level. She tries to estimate how far, but it is too minor. Too small a variation, though there should be none. She checks the flight run numbers, puts them to one side, and opens the first envelope for the day. A run of vertical shots far from the Henge. Distance and distraction put the change she thought she saw out of her mind, and she lets herself fall into the silvered fields.

~

By close of day Marissa has worked her way through several runs, none of them showing any sign of parchmarks or earthworks. On some the vegetation is too dense, on others the weather too poor, or the light in the wrong place. She works through lunch, and snacks through the afternoon, until the wall-mounted clock shudders to hometime.

Clearing the desk, she pulls the two photos back under the twin lenses of the stereoscope, slides them around until the two images of the Henge overlap, then conjoin, then become one.

There is no doubt now. The Henge in the decades-old photograph has changed; the stones plunged through the vegetation. She tries to estimate the depth by the shadow, and comes up with a figure of one metre. The descent is rapid. She looks around the room where she works.

Concrete walls are hidden behind posters still colourful with no sunlight to strip them of their vibrancy. Not for the first time she feels the isolation press upon her. Her thoughts are only hers and not something she can share, but this is something that needs another person. Her eyes might finally be failing. The view flattening or distorting. She puts the defective world into a new manila envelope, picks up her coat and closes her door.

~

The project director is distant, both in location and personality. She climbs the stairs past rooms of colleagues who she rarely sees and only vaguely knows, until she reaches the office flooded with all the daylight hers never gets.

Her knock is tentative, as is the voice that answers her. She opens the door and goes in.

Bill Wyatt is an extruded figure of a man whose body extends far beyond his own knowledge of himself. He drapes across his chair and desk as if one single piece of furniture cannot contain him. When he looks up, she thinks his neck is going to sever from the weight of his head.

"You could have just phoned." While his limbs are overlong, his social skills are shrunken and small. Something to be carried out at distance, like the photos that they both search.

"This needed to be in person, and I thought it important enough to visit."

He looks toward her hand as if nothing so small could be so important.

"A new monument type? Fill in the records, and bring it to my attention the usual way."

She shakes her head.

"The photos are changing," she says, and places the envelope in front of him.

He unfolds the flap and takes out the two square photos, clears a space on the crowded desk and places them side by side. Turning them over, he examines the back of the paper, then the images themselves. Holds them up, looking for laminating along the edge.

"Not the physical photo, but what is being shown," Marissa says.

"The image is deteriorating?"

"The images are changing."

From behind him he recovers a small stereoscope, folding out the wire legs. Every movement is slow and exact. She cannot decide if this is because the precision is important to him or because he hopes she will take back the problem and leave.

Once the device is in place above the photos, she watches him shift them back and forth until he is satisfied.

"Focus on the Henge," she says without being invited to speak. She spends too long working on her own to worry about niceties.

He looks up, his breath steaming the lenses, pauses, cleans them with an old rag, then searches the landscape once more.

"So what has changed? What am I not seeing that you are?"

"The stones. They're sinking into the ground."

He looks again, and she wonders how he can see anything straight when shaking his head. Taking his time, he folds the stereoscope away once more, and leans back in his chair that probably costs more than the whole contents of her office.

"In this job, your eyes are your real tool," he tells her, as if she doesn't know. "You have to look after them. We can arrange an optician's test, if you think it would help?"

She stares at him for a moment. There is nothing wrong with her eyes, and they both know it. She will not give him a route to force her out.

"I must be mistaken," she lies. "I'll just get on with the other runs."

He hands her back the envelope and two photographs.

"Please let us know if there is anything we can do."

Down in her office, she tries to resist looking once more, but she needs to leave the photos out anyway, and the stereoscope is just there.

Two of the stones have completely disappeared, leaving nothing but black shadows. Four more are only just visible. The deceit of the stereoscope makes her think she can plunge her hand down into the shafts which now pepper the centre of the Henge. She shudders and pushes the photos together so the earthworks blur and slide out of view.

~

The next morning Marissa arrives early, makes her coffee and places it on the desk, far enough away from the stereoscope that the caffeinated steam will not opaque the lenses.

The two photos are still there, laid at odd angles to each other amidst the piles of notebooks and unopened archival envelopes. She picks up the first, holds it at a distance for a moment, then stares at it in isolation without its fraternal twin.

The stones are still visible, still just white pills of limestone balanced on a raised platform of scorched dirt, low summer sun turning them luminescent in the photo's silver nitrate. She places it down and picks up the second, taken moments later by the camera slung under the plane. The same. All six stones lying prone upon the land as they had for millennia while people were born and died and paid them no attention.

She has five minutes until she needs to start work properly. She opens the glasses case that holds the stereoscope, folds out the legs and shifts the two photos until they swim, doppler, and settle into place.

The holes are still there. Deeper now. All six stones disappeared down shafts the same size and shape as each hewn rock. Tendrils of nausea branch out from her stomach, through her arms and legs until she can no longer stand. The hollows look gouged, too much like a skull collapsed by the impact of heavy aluminium falling from height. She pulls the wastepaper basket close and vomits into the thin plastic rubbish bag. Wiping her mouth, she catches sight of Simon's photo and her stomach contracts once more.

The photos are still in place. She braces herself and looks again.

Something else has changed. Where before the voids were edged in raw peat, decaying plants of three thousand years exposed by the stones' descent, now the lip of each hole glistens with something damp and fibrous. It seems to seep upwards against gravity, covering the nearest plant life. Even at the distance created by the photographs, there is movement there. She separates the photos and sits back. Picks them up in turn. The stones are still in place. Unchanged. Unmoving. She hesitates before gazing at them once more, as if she is trying to convince herself that this is not her problem. That this is not her concern. She fails.

~

The photocopier is on the second floor. She is first in. First to use the giant block of yellowed plastic that stands between two office doors.

The plug is hidden, and she scrapes her hand reaching for the on switch. Inside, the device grumbles to life, and she places the photos in turn upon the glass.

For each one she makes multiple copies, some lighter, some darker, and when she returns to her small windowless room she pairs them in many combinations, including with the original photos. The stones remain on the surface, until she reunites the originals.

~

The knock is soon followed by the door opening. An act of ownership over the space. An act of ownership over her.

Bill Wyatt comes in and stands beside her. She digs her fingernails into her wrists to stop the words, because this is his space too and her time is his time, or that's what he wants to convince her of.

"I came to see how things were progressing."

He glances toward Simon's photo. She wonders if he still blames her for reporting what happened. She started working inside because she couldn't face going on site anymore. Bill started working inside because she told the truth.

"A lot to do," she says, her fingers still on the two photos.

"I can take those with me if they're distracting you," he says, nodding toward the desk.

"No." She snatches her hand away a little too fast, spreading the photocopies across her desk. An act of concealment out in full view.

Bill picks up five envelopes stuffed with photo runs and stacks them in the centre of her desk.

"I want these transcribed by the end of the month, or we might have to have a talk about your productivity."

She nods, picks one up and pretends to look at the information sticker on the outside.

"I might need to do a site visit," she says, making sure she does not look toward the pair of photos showing the Henge. If she defocuses her eyes, will the holes manifest, like some kind of magic eye picture? The photos both distract her and tempt her to turn her gaze.

"Are you sure you're ready?"

She nods and knows it is a little too slow. Gives him chance to use her wellbeing as an excuse.

"We'll talk about it when you've finished those," he says, nodding toward the unopened manila envelopes threatening to topple across her workspace.

"I'll keep you updated," she says, and turns away from him toward the work. Behind her, the door shuts. It is only when he has gone she notices he has taken the two photos with him.

Her first thought is to wait until he leaves and collect them from his desk, but his office will be locked, and the receptionist will have too many questions for her, and too many answers for Bill the following day. She glances toward the photo of Simon, unpins it, and puts it in her pocket.

~

"I didn't mean to be rude," the receptionist says, hesitating before unhooking the key fob from the board. "It's just you've never asked for a pool car before, and it caught me off-guard."

Marissa reads the car registration number on the paper tag and drops it in her pocket.

"Which car is it?" she asks, running her finger over the key. She hasn't had a reason to do a field visit in a long time. She glances toward the door as if the outside is another world, not somewhere she lives for the other sixteen hours a day.

"You'll need to sign out," the receptionist says. Each little wall of bureaucracy is another part of her castle to defend.

Marissa writes her name and pushes the clipboard back.

"It's the white Mondeo, to the left of the entrance. Make sure you leave it with a full tank."

~

Marissa parks the car in a gravelled lay-by, barely any room to get out without stepping into the road. There are no stiles or gates, so instead Marissa climbs the wall, finding steps where there are none, hands coated in moss and thin soil.

Walking across the moor is like holding the hand of a dying aunt. The sensation that all signs of life are pretence. Paper thin. Everything just below the surface hollowed out by some unseen infection.

The day is warm, but the wind takes away any heat. Unsettles the insects so they swarm into the air, and she needs to walk through them. There is no path to follow, but she knows where to go. Even though the landscape now surrounds her, she has studied every square metre many times. Even with the moor covered in heather, she can find her way across. Somewhere to her left a grouse breaks cover and she starts. Pauses to catch her breath. Continues.

The Henge itself is hermetic, any view of the inside hidden by the banks that seem to pulse and constrict as Marissa approaches. She stares over her shoulder toward the road. A white van is climbing the hill. A flash of the stable world that shimmers and drops below the stone walls as it enters a dip in the road. She continues walking.

Grasping the heather, she climbs the banks, stable underfoot though it still undulates. Standing on top she is more exposed. The scent of heather and decaying vegetation is far below her now. None of that matters. She is gazing into the centre of the earthwork. Into six deep shafts edged in strands, grey like silver suspended in gelatine, fibrous like matted hair. She is gazing into an event she tries not to remember.

It's the sound that stays with her the most. The noise the aluminium platform made as it slid from the scaffold, careered down, forcing splinters of bone so far that they were found embedded in Simon's tongue. The sound of Bill Wyatt pleading with her not to say anything, even while he was still up the scaffold photo tower. Even while his foot still hung in the air above nothing – apart from the man dying on the grass below.

She wonders if the stones will continue sinking until they melt in the magma that lies at the heart of the earth. There is no heat rising from the pits. The air above the Henge is cold and does not still. She walks down the inside of the bank. Lets gravity do most of the work. The strands laid across the bracken look like seaweed. More bulbous than she was expecting. She wants to feel one against her skin but resists the urge. Instead, she walks as close to the holes as she dares and gazes inside.

"It wasn't my fault, you know."

Bill Wyatt stands on the bank, buffeted by the wind. Marissa steps back from the edge of the nearest hole.

"None of it was my fault. He should have moved."

She has to shield her eyes from the sun to look at him.

"You were too impatient. He didn't have a chance."

"I didn't ask for you to work on this project, either. Not because you're not good enough, but because I didn't want to punish you," he lies.

"You didn't want me to work on this project so you didn't have to see Simon's memory every day. That's the exact reason I made sure I got the job."

She wonders if the stones are still descending. If she jumps, will she land upon one? Will she lie there, bone shattered and starving as it descends through the planet?

"Why did you have to make things worse? Someone died that day." She sees tears glisten on his cheeks, soon dried by the breeze.

"He had a name!"

Bill stumbles down the bank, nearly falling several times, before he reaches the foot of the overgrown ditch. Marissa backs up onto the platform at the centre, stepping carefully around the holes.

"I know he has a name," Bill says. "Do you think I can forget? I see him every night. I see the hole in his skull every night. The sound it made when they pulled out the metal. Every night." He follows her into the centre of the Henge. She glances back and steps further between the holes. The silver fibres seem to notice her passing.

"And then there you are to remind me. Every day. Every time I see you, you wear that same fucking expression. You don't have to carry around the guilt."

"You're right," she says. "I don't. I just have to carry around his memory."

His expression changes from some kind of contrition to anger. He reaches forward and tries to step toward her.

The fibres from the pits have grasped his feet while he was talking, and when he tries to move, he falls. Slowly, they spread. A bulbous root-mat anchoring itself in his skin. The thin-walled blisters burst against his limbs, and as each one erupts, he screams. The fibres ignore her. Let her step down into the ditch where she watches him slowly become coated and scorched as the fibres constrict. Force their way down his throat and into his eyes.

She does not turn away.

Once there is no more Bill to see, the fibres withdraw, drag themselves back, and when they need to return to several holes they shatter him, each clump dragging a different piece out of sight below the earth.

Marissa walks to the edge and peers inside. There is no sign of the silvered weeds. No sign of Bill.

She considers jumping. Let the void take her too, but that is not an option. She now knows her role. To witness the deaths and carry the memories in silence. She wonders if the stones will return. It does not matter. Her hand goes to the photo in her pocket. She runs her fingers along the creases. Simon is gone forever, and the death of Bill will not return him. All she can do is carry the memory and let him live a little within.

God in
a Box

I found a God in a small wooden box. No, not God as in Jesus, Billy Graham, Praise the Lord, but *a* God.

It was during an excavation, hidden on some stairs and covered by 200 years of soil. I know I should have handed it in. It goes against every instinct and professional standard. But could you imagine the finds department.

"Small Find 104: Deity 250mm x 400mm x 30mm. Material: Wood; sand; the light of a spring dawn; the anguished cry of a newborn second son, tied together with a cracked piece of leather."

Never mind the problem of conservation.

You're not getting this are you?

It's not a statue of a God, it is A God.

What do you mean what is the box like?

I tell you I have a small God living in my desk and you ask me what the box is like. I bet if Moses had told you about the burning bush, you would have asked what kind of bush. It's a very plain wooden box with a rusted lock, and slightly creaking hinges

Do you know I've never asked what it's the God of.

Oh yes we do talk. Its voice is whispery, sort of like a warm breeze on an Autumn's morning.

Well it can't be a Weather God because, well, look at the past few months.

I don't think it's a God of Luck, although I did win that ten pounds on the lottery.

A God of Love? It doesn't look very romantic.

What has changed?

Well there are some differences. Everything seems brighter – colour, sunlight. We were in the woods last week and the colours just flowed out of the bark.

And flavours. Everything I eat tastes like the first meal of a starving man.

Yes I am noticing other things: figures flitting in the corners of my eye, and voices, voices between sleeping and waking.

Everything seems, well, enhanced. Sharper, more defined.

When I leave it at home everything is slightly greyer, but if I put it in my pocket I can hear the whispers under the traffic and the souls of the creatures in the limestone.

Sacrifices? Well it did come up once but it said that I didn't have to worry about that for now. It would keep track of what sacrifices I owed it and we could talk about it another time.

# Dirt Upon My Skin

Sally noticed Campbell had gone, and the surveying pole fell from her cramped grip to smash beyond repair upon the kerb. Moments earlier they had been alone together in the disowned housing estate. Now Campbell's hi-vis jacket was not in sight. Sally and the tripod-legged Level stood at opposite ends of the deserted street.

Shouldering the pole, she unclipped the two-way radio from her belt, pressing the push-to-talk button, still warm from their last exchange.

"Stop fucking around," she said. They had worked together long enough and often enough. "If you want to sneak off for a piss, let me know." She let go of the switch and waited for the reply that didn't come.

Either side, empty houses canyoned over her, walls salt-stained and windows blinded. She pressed the button again.

"Seriously, stop dicking around. We need to get this benchmark transferred. The machines are arriving in the morning."

No answer. Campbell's bag lay on the floor beside the Level, the notebook he used to write down measurements left on top. She picked it up and shielded her eyes from the harsh sun. The page was blank. While she knelt amongst grit and used needles, he had made no attempt to take a measurement. She stared down at the tiny spirit bubble in its emerald green liquid. The thing wasn't even set up properly.

"Fuck's sake." She picked up the radio once more. "Me and you are going to have words, Campbell."

The equipment was too valuable to leave, and there was no way she was waiting for him to return.

Garstang Estate was vast, one of the biggest in Europe when it was built. Row upon row of back-to-backs fused together, sharing bricks like conjoined twins shared arteries. Long avenues and narrow back lanes. The whole lot bought up to be cleared for new development in 2006. And in 2008? Left to rot when the money markets were mined out from underneath.

Six years later and no progress. Windows and doors were shuttered to keep out the growers. No matter how many activists shouted the houses were still good enough to live in, the buildings were caught in confusions of ownership too complex for any single entity to unravel. Silent streets. Abandoned. Forgotten.

Static bubbled from the speaker. She put the Level into its polystyrene cradle and unclipped the radio again. The red LED glowed to show someone on the paired handset speaking. The static did not clear. No words were audible.

"If you can hear me, say something," she said, cutting across the broadcast. When she finished the red light had blinked out once more. She was alone. No one was listening.

For an hour she waited in case he returned, walking up and down the short length of street, then sitting a while on the kerb, tarmac too hot to touch. To distract herself she peered into the backyards. Rats ate dead crows now there were no binbags to rip open.

Campbell was not returning. She was not going to achieve anything by herself, and the car had aircon.

The tripod strap dug into her shoulder, prongs banging against her shins. The small carpark lay beyond the fence on the far side of the estate. She checked one pocket for the wrench to open the razor wire topped gate. Checked the other pocket for the car key.

Working alone didn't bother her. Being deserted did. She stopped every few houses to check the radio. Nothing came after that first eruption of static. She thought about turning it off to save batteries, but what if Campbell was in trouble? Wandered off and concussed himself? She caught her breath once more, hefted the equipment and walked on toward the estate's core.

The playing field was big enough to hold a football pitch and some rusted climbing frames.

On one side the slight rise of earthworks they were here to survey.

At one time the Iron Age hillfort extended its embrace through the land now thronged with houses. Sally had seen the 19th-century Ordnance Survey maps, the triple bank and ditch still roping the escarpment.

She remembered tracing that ribbon of ramparts with her finger during the rushed Desk Based Assessment of the site.

The rest were long gone. Scraped and scoured by the flattening plough long before the streets were planned out. The single crease of earth on the playing field was the last survivor of that once majestic structure. An artefact of ownership, preserved by chance. Now even that was to be lost, ruptured with steel to sling mobile phone signals from one part of the city to the other.

She climbed the slope and stood on top, the turf skin underfoot wearing old blackened scars of fires. Pivoted as lightly as she could. Listened for steps in the streets. Any movement would be Campbell's. No one else was in the estate.

The house was fifty metres away and stood out from all the others only because there was no shutter across the door. The windows were still heavy grilled, gridded steel nail-gunned in place, red painted door an exposed bruise.

She hesitated. They were not out to do a building survey, though of course they could, and they were not there to investigate anything beyond the small length of surviving earthwork. But.

That word was sour wine on Sally's tongue. She checked her phone. Still no signal. Maybe Campbell had decided to get out of the sun. Not that he had the tools to unfasten one of the shutters. Maybe he just got lucky. Felt too hot and got lucky.

The stone around the door casing was smooth. No sign of any bolts. No sign any shutter had been put up at all. The only disturbance was a clumped smear of red on the doorstep. She ran a single finger through the mark. Ochre. They had found some in a burial across town earlier in the year.

Putting her ear to the wood, Sally listened. There was no electricity in the estate any more, all the power turned off eight years ago. If there was a growing operation inside, they would be using generators. Generators were loud and disturbed the air like summer storms, but the house was silent. No reek of diesel or dope. She waited a moment to try the door, and turned on her phone torch.

Nothing had been touched. Sally had spent days working in abandoned houses. Hours clocked up sidestepping voids left by stolen floorboards. Avoiding piles of rotten pigeons as she sketched original architectural features. Photographed bricked-in windows. Tried to record important plaster decoration cleaved by the theft of copper wiring and central heating pipes.

Through the red door everything was in place as if the last residents were coming back from work at the end of the day. Curtains still on rails and bulbs still in their fittings. Curiosity got the better of her and she flicked the light switch. Nothing happened. Apart from the pale blue phone light she stayed in darkness.

"Campbell." Her voice trespassed through the air and came back an interloper. There was no one else. She opened the front room door.

There had long been rumours of empty houses on the Garstang used to hide dead bodies. But why any of the city's gangsters would risk discovery during demolition was beyond her. The harbour's schools of fish were hungry and efficient.

Twin piles of soil reached walls on both sides of the lounge, tipping away from the hole in the centre. She looked back the way she'd come, then down at her signal-less phone. The Police should deal with this, she told herself, but what to say?

Dead bodies went with the job. This one would just be more recent than the usual Romano-British skeletons she excavated. More soft tissue. Fresher. She directed the torchlight down and stared into the hole.

The pit was a metre deep and about the same wide, undercutting the floorboards. A single horse foreleg jagged across the middle. On one side a spread of Iron Age pottery sherds, inclusions glittering in the black, oxygen-starved clay like galaxies. The far end of the pit base was hidden beneath a barn owl, wings splayed and pinned with damp-softened wooden pegs. She crouched down, gripping onto the splintered floorboards, and leant over. Blood clotted along the severed limb. She directed the torch light toward the owl. In the harsh glow from her cellphone its chest feathers rose and fell.

She ignored the calf leg, and the dying bird of prey, trying to look at the room with professional eyes. The pit cut (sharp break of slope-top; irregular sides with steep gradient; gradual break of slope-base; uneven base), the texture of the soil (silty clay with occasional small limestone inclusions), and the colour (brown yellow, though the artificial light was misleading).

The stench of torn muscle reached Sally, dragging her attention back to the leg. Exposed joints twitched as tendons dried out. The owl was still. Reed-like bones collapsed against the dirt. Sally leant against the wall to catch her breath, and ran into the deserted street.

The door opposite was exposed. Frosted glass bisected by a single crack. She stared toward the sanctuary of the playing field, then remembered Campbell.

Free of brickdust, the doorstep was once more marked in ochre. A thick, red, mineral line and circle on the rough stone. She tried the door, the handle's bubbled chrome against her skin. It opened, catching on the distended carpet beyond.

The broken glass let in enough light to see by. Enough for Sally to set her feet between the dead woodlice littering the floor.

"Campbell!" She shouted up the stairs. No answer came. "Campbell! Are you in here?"

Still no answer. It was possible that the teams securing the buildings had cut corners, but she hadn't noticed the unshuttered entrances on their way into the estate that morning. The house creaked contractions as it inhaled heat from the now-open entrance. Wood twisted. Plaster tried to collapse in upon itself.

Kneeling, she ran a hand along the skirting board, wood softened enough to let her press through to the wall behind. She wiped her hand on her jeans.

In the kitchen the pit stretched from the laminate worktop to the cooker. Spoil heaps collapsed into the sink. Taps dripped rusting water through rotten washers, small patches of dirt turning to mud. Sally brushed against the edge of the pit cut and turned her torch on the base.

The femurs had been picked clean. Correction, she thought. The femurs had been scraped clean, heavy knife cuts around the cartilage. In the centre a rib cage, thin bones broken during splaying. Ropes of nettle fibre knotted around the remaining vertebrae. An intact bowl balanced where the head would be, the rim thinned with finger pressed decoration. Climbing down, she reached into her back pocket for her trowel and scraped out a sample of the contents. A thick rendered fat, spattered with small pieces of rotten meat, congealed on the metal blade.

She stepped back, heel slipping, and collapsed the pit edge. Only then did she uncover feathers lining the hole behind a thin layer of backfill. Magpie feathers, quills packed with the same fat in the bowl. She squeezed the grease into her palm and smeared it on the wall.

Outside again she bowed her head, the taste of her own stomach on her lips, and stared at nothing apart from the pavement. Despite the scorching sun, the wind had got up and banged the two open doors in their frames. The sound multiplied. Eight more houses were now open, none showing any trace of ever being shuttered.

Picking one at random, she ran over and opened the exposed entrance. The air inside was thick with the reek of dried cooking fat coating the walls, wallpaper underneath discoloured by nicotine and mildew. She did not enter, stopping only to stare at the ochre mark on the step; three circles linked by three lines.

The next was across the road. She pulled the door toward her.

The pit was just inside the hallway, spoil tipping away into the darkness. Cattle forelegs were arranged on the base so they crossed just above the hooves, skin flayed back. Petals of uncured hide, blowflies laying their young between fat and bone. She stumbled out again. The radio crackled on her hip. She turned up the volume and held it against her ear.

The drumming was distorted by dirt ground into the speaker. The sound fibrous and thin. Fading in and out, signal not quite strong enough. She heard the echo from one of the terraces opposite. A dull rhythm, beaten out on stretched skin. The other handset was nearby. Inside one of the houses. Campbell was nearby.

The drumming got louder as she approached. Constant and complex. Repetitive. Insistent. She walked up to the unshuttered doors. Nothing came from within. The noise was elsewhere. She walked further down the street. Another opened house. Turned the handle and listened. The drumming continued. Still no closer. She stayed still. The noise came from the neighbouring building.

The house was still fastened tight against looting, no wood or glass visible behind the grills. The sound continued behind the walls. She pressed the push-to-talk button, and held the radio to her mouth.

"Campbell, can you hear me?" Her own voice came back at her from inside, muffled by the thick brick walls. Not an interloper this time, but a prisoner, trapped by the emptiness within the house. She did not speak again. Each word she heard made her want to run and keep on running.

Across the road was yet another unfastened house. Still no brick dust. The same red ochre marks scrawled on the entrance. Concentric circles rippling out to the step edge. The door was already open. She gripped either side of the frame.

Stepped inside.

The downstairs rooms had been knocked together sometime in the past. The pit was the largest she'd seen so far, cut reaching all four walls. Any spoil taken upstairs, she guessed. She had no idea how deep the hole was. The whole thing was covered in severed crow wings. Hundreds of them overlapped each over, laid carefully so their extended feathers did not entwine. She fumbled with her phone and turned on the torch. The light reflected off the barbs' tallowed surfaces. In places the stack of wings was lower in the ground, not reaching up to the floor. She stretched out her foot. Kicked them to one side.

The hi-vis waistcoat was stained where blood had pooled down Campbell's neck, waist riding up as she moved the severed overburden. His skin hung loose in strips, petalled like the cattle limbs. Ribboned fat scraped from underneath. Sally tried to think of it as just another burial, just another body. On her radio the drumming got louder, echoing in the room. She threw the wings over her shoulder, not caring any more where they landed.

More feathers lay under him, several broken pot rims arranged around his hands. A single boar's tusk forced into his mouth. Two more through his eye sockets, now holding nothing more than balls of hay. His arms were severed at the wrist, hands clasped together.

There was no way to save him. There was nothing left to save. He was a collection of finds. A burial record to be written. Context sheets to be filled in. A plan to be drawn and levels to be taken. One more of millions of dead to rot in the ground, names forgotten. He was just another collection of finds. Another burial to be excavated. Another collection of finds. She repeated the words to herself like a liturgy.

The feathers left thick grease across her palms. She tried wiping it away on her jeans. Her boot slipped on the fill, and Campbell shifted as if disturbed in sleep.

Unable to stare at his skinned face any more, she climbed out, ran into the street and vomited into the gutter.

The house opposite had no shutters now. All of them gone. Windows exposed and door open. She ran her hand across the pale bricks. Not a single nail scar anywhere. The sills were marked in red ochre. The door too. Inside, she heard the radio screech feedback. Drumming louder now. A single horn blown. Mournful. Hollow.

If she got the radio it was proof. Proof that Campbell had gone missing and she'd found him. No need to disturb the burial. Easy. Just enter one more empty house. Entered many empty houses in her career. All full of dead birds.

These were just more houses full of dead birds. Abandoned. Vandalised. Just dead birds.

Sally went inside. Through the first door. Through the second. Within the front room, the pit was vast. Spoilheaps stacked against the chimney breast and covered the gas fire. Limestone bedrock shoveled into the open-plan kitchen. The staircase. She stood on the edge of the hole and stared in. The pit was empty. No bird wings. No cattle bones. No joints of meat. No pottery. Nothing. A scoured cut sloping down to a smooth U shaped base. She stared around the room looking for the dead. Looking for the rubbish. Looking for the corpses. Behind her the doors clicked shut.

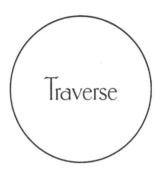

Traverse

Note:

*K. Patrick Glover mentioned this project to me because of my interest in Forteana. A couple of weeks later I met with an old friend from my archaeology degree who now works for a university archive. While we were having a beer the Ilchester Tunnel came up in conversation. Once they realised it was the one in Maryland not Somerset they told me about a research project studying 19th century temporary worker camps across Western Europe and the United States. It seems that the project stalled after a training excavation in Ellicot City went wrong. Although she couldn't get me the project records she was able to let me see the site diary and the personal diary of the archaeologist in charge of the work, Jenny Calburn. I'm not sure exactly what happened here, (Jenny has recorded a lot of unprofessional practices and there seems to have been a real tension between her and Ewan), but I passed them on to K.*

*Patrick Glover. I thought they could add a bit*
*of background to the history of the tunnel.*

*Steve Toase*

~

Missing Person Unit
National Crime Agency
Public Liaison

Dr Samuel Brentford
Head of Dept
Department of Archaeology
and Prehistory

Dear Dr Brentford,
Thank you for your recent letter
requesting an update into the case of
Jenny Calbourn. I can tell you that as of
this point in time we have made no further
progress. As a result we are pausing our
investigations, and have returned the
site records mentioned in your letter,
including both the site diary and Jenny
Calburn's personal diary.
    With kind regards,
    PC Faith Mayweather
    Public Liaison Officer

~

## Jenny Calburn's Personal Diary
## 15th October

Not a good start. First all the hassle getting the equipment through customs (something that the university were supposed to have sorted out). Then when we do get through and get all the surveying kit cleared there's no-one from the Historical Society waiting to meet us. Ewan was even more snappy than usual. I know that he doesn't want to be here. It's not my fault that the Archaeology Department don't think I'm senior enough to run the excavation on my own. Like I told him, sexism affects us all.

We finally managed to get a minibus taxi sorted out and get to the accommodation (at least the university managed not to mess that up). I'm just writing this now before I get some sleep. Jetlag is kicking me to bits. I'm glad we programmed in a rest day tomorrow, but I want to get started!

## Jenny Calburn's Personal Diary
## 16th October

Slept late. Far too late.

Still no sign of our contact. I've tried ringing the local historical society, but no answer. I've told the students to have some time off. Go and familiarise themselves with the town. Ewan wasn't too happy about that. I believe his exact words were,

"The last thing we need is that lot laid up with hangovers." A bit hypocritical, considering.

**Update**

The local contact Sarah McSanders finally turned up at 6:30pm, full of apologies. Barely stopped longer than five minutes. Some kind of ongoing family crisis, but promised to meet us on the site at 8am tomorrow.

## Site Diary
### 17th October

First day on site.

Contact Sarah MacSanders met us at the entrance,

All required permits to allow work to begin in order.

Introductory talk about the history of the location delivered, with a focus on the relationship between the camp and the nearby tunnel/bridge.

Short tour of the area directly around the site to put the project in context.

Health and safety talk delivered

First job tomorrow is to clear the undergrowth that is obscuring the earthworks.

## Jenny Calburn's Personal Diary
### 17th October

I thought Ewan was going to lose it. There's always one student. He should know that by now. One who chooses to mouth off. When Sarah had finished talking about the background of the area, and asked if there was any questions, James Sandhaven put his hand up. I didn't show it, but groaned inside. Anyway, he started talking about how he'd been reading up on the area, while Sarah nodded along, then he pointed behind us in the vague direction of the tunnel and said,

"I've heard something about Peeping Tom. What do you know about him?"

For a moment she looked like she was going to say something, then smiled and muttered about paying attention to real history rather than rumours. Ewan ended the whole thing quickly, before any of the other students decided to play up. I mean they're only first years. Barely out of school, and they just need to let off some steam. Tomorrow we have some local volunteers joining us. That should help keep things a bit calmer.

We moved all the equipment into the house we're using for a site hut. I was led to believe that there would be power, but there's no evidence of this. No time to hire a generator either. I really need to have a word with the department. Sending us halfway around the world only partially resourced. At least they packed the step down voltage convertors.

It was a good opportunity to observe the students actually doing some work together. Usual mixture of first years with a handful of second years supervising. Most just here to get a free trip because it sounded more interesting than doing their practical in a field in Doncaster. Some keen (maybe a bit too keen), others lazy as fuck. We'll see how they cope with the site clearance tomorrow.

**Site Diary**
**18th October**

Arrived at site early. Divided into three work groups to enable us to circulate students around different tasks.

Morning spent cutting back vegetation.

Navvy camp foundations starting to emerge.

Starting to define stone footings for Navvy camp's more permanent buildings.

Once all undergrowth removed and stacked, initial site photos taken.

Basic training in using the cameras delivered to each group.

Students started recording visible features

During this stage some graffiti was found carved into the stonework. At first glance they seemed to be surveying marks; a circle with a line running through them. While Ewan led the teams in further scrub clearance I created a photographic record of these marks.

By the end of the day had identified over 27 spread across the site.

Three first years were trained in locating the surveying benchmark to bring in for the topographic survey working from the plans provided. All the work they did back in England was using Ordnance Survey benchmarks so it took a while to find the US Geodetic Survey plaque just inside the tunnel.

### Jenny Calburn's Personal Diary
### 18th October

I sometimes wonder why I bothered getting Ewan this job. He has absolutely no interest in teaching even the basics, and his mood is worse because it's not his project. I know that smarts for him. He doesn't say anything directly of course, but watching the way he talks to the students, and gets distracted to the point of doing nothing, it's pretty obvious where his head is at. Me finding the graffiti really got his back up. He missed out on funding for the project back in the UK. Again, he won't say anything directly. Won't talk about it. I tried mentioning it once and he changed the subject so fast I thought he was going to give himself whiplash.

We at least made some progress with the site. All the scrub is cleared and stacked at the side ready for burning, and we've found the survey point so can bring in a temporary bench mark tomorrow.

I took James Somerfeld, Kath Bryce, and Gemma Tyson to do the surveying. I'll be honest, not because they have the most aptitude, though they're not the worst three on the site, but because they seem to be well liked and it always helps to get to know those ones first.

When we got to the tunnel, there was a load of giggling and I heard Peeping Tom get mentioned again.

I know they're technically adults, but I've still got a duty of care to them, and it's the sort of situation ripe for the girls to be taken advantage of. Turns out it's some kind of urban legend connected to the tunnel. It took me at least four times of asking before Kath finally told me what it was all about. Turns out it's some kind of local Bloody Mary variation. Challenge test. That sort of thing. Stare down the tunnel for an hour, see Peeping Tom. At midnight. I wonder how many of these stories are still going?

When we got back to the accommodation a few of us ended up sitting outside talking about these stories from when we were growing up. Even Ewan joined in, telling us how he stood in front of a mirror at Primary School reciting the Lord's Prayer backwards to try and make the Devil appear, but nothing happened. I told them about my American cousin who made us do Bloody Mary, and then ran out of the house when I crept into her bedroom at night wearing an old Halloween mask.

We were a bit loud, to be fair, but I was still surprised when the hotel manager came up and tore strips off us. Not because we were disturbing the other guests, but because of what we were talking about.

I suggested to everyone we go into my room and carry on talking there, but the heart had gone out of it.

### Site Diary
### 19th October

Met Sarah MacSanders on site.

Unfortunately the local volunteers we were hoping for are not available now. We have a large enough team of students so were able to set them up and working.

First task, clean up all the stonework for proper recording. Once that's done we can decide the best way of carrying out the topographic survey. This decision is student led.

The students decided that a series of transects two metres apart would give us a sufficient density of points to capture the detail.

Traverse from the survey point to the site to establish the temporary benchmark completed as a training exercise. Ewan took a second team to complete the traverse back. We repeated this training task to train everyone in using the Total Station Theodolite independently by the end of the day.

Unfortunately a storm came in during this stage. Conditions were completely unworkable and we had to abandon site.

Back at the accommodation I delivered a talk on the differences and similarities in American and British navvy camps of the time.

### Jenny Calburn's Personal Diary
### 19th October

Today was a complete wash out. We got a small amount done before the skies opened, but not really enough to justify any of the effort put in. We had to abandon by 2pm, so we didn't even get the survey started. To top it all Sarah MacSanders now tells me that the local volunteers have bailed on us, and she admits she's fairly new to the area, so all that local knowledge I was hoping to tap into is not available. I raised my voice. I'm not proud of it, but what do people expect? This project is turning into one broken promise after another. We were meant to be doing a social history of the navvy camp. Trying to find the living relatives through informal conversations and then include that research in our project.

MacSanders has suggested she can speak to some local families, see if they are willing to be interviewed by the students, but that's not my research approach, and they're just not going to open up in the same way.

## Jenny Calburn's Personal Diary
### 20th October 3am

It's three in the morning, and I'm sat here fucking furious. Ewan has just left after telling me he left the Total Station set up at the tunnel when the weather closed in. Several thousand pounds worth of equipment just left there, in the middle of fucking nowhere. Switched on too! So the battery will be fucked. The spare is charged, but I've no idea if it will work, because of course he couldn't remember if he put on the rain cover.

Honestly, I'm sick of him. I'm sick of his willful incompetence. How do you forget that you've left the survey equipment set up? He asked if I wanted him to go and get it now, but there didn't seem much point. We're back on site in a few hours, and if it's going to be stolen then it will have already happened. I don't even know if the liability insurance will cover this. That's the department's only Total Station and I had to fight tooth and nail for them to let me bring it over. It's not his reputation on the line. At least we didn't get started on the survey so there's no data to lose. I'm so tempted just to abandon the lot of them, climb on a Greyhound and get lost somewhere.

### Site Diary
### October 20th

The weather is much better today.

We had an unfortunate incident where the Total Station was left out on site overnight during the bad weather. However, after a new battery was fitted everything seems to be working OK. There are some anomalous readings on the Data-logger, but we can remove those at a later stage.

Once certain the Total Station was working we began the topographic survey of the site. The aim of this stage of the project is to allow the students to:

- each have a turn operating the equipment and working on the staff
- learn the restrictions and limitations of each part of the process
- learn that surveying is a partnership where the person holding the staff is just as important if not more so
- learn decisions have more influence on the quality of the survey

To facilitate this we're logging each transect with the initials of students taking the readings so that when we process the data they can compare their accuracy.

We laid out the test pits.

Our permits are pretty strict. We are only allowed to excavate a total of ten 1m x 1m test pits across the camp.

We can have two students working on each test pit and rotate them out to work on the Total Station, so that they gain experience of carrying out both topographic survey and excavation.

Ewan is supervising the excavation side, training the students in context recording, planning and section drawing.

I'm working on the survey.

By lunch we've completed several transects. All pairs have so far correctly identified a lot of detail is getting missed by taking points every metre, so we're increasing the density of points recorded allowing a much more detailed survey.

### Jenny Calburn's Personal Diary
### 20th October

We actually made progress today, opening up several test pits and getting the topographic survey started. On the whole the students are enthusiastic, and learning quickly, which is the point of the exercise, I guess. I'm still worried about the Total Station. There seems to be a weird smudge inside the lens. I'm hoping that water hasn't got in and damaged the optics. I mentioned it to Ewan, but he just shrugged and said something about it all coming out in the wash.

When I got back to the accommodation I decided to download the data. Belt and braces. Everything seems OK in the datalog. The only issue is a series of anomalous readings between the initial traverse bringing in the temporary benchmark and the topographic survey. Normally we use a letter code so we can identify what we're surveying, but these are prefixed by Ө

### Jenny Calburn's Personal Diary
### 21st October 2am

I couldn't sleep. Something about those readings. There's only three of them, but they don't make sense. I went through all the menus on the Total Station and there isn't a way to even generate that symbol. Then I, finally, checked the time and date on the readings. They were all taken just after midnight when the Total Station was left out at the tunnel.

Ewan wasn't asleep when I knocked on his door. He pretended to be, but I'd heard him moving around before I knocked.

When he answered the door I showed him the laptop, and pointed out what he should be looking at.

"So?"

That was his answer. His only answer.

"Someone messed around with the Total Station after you left it out."

He took the laptop off me and peered at the screen. I'm sure I smelt whiskey on his breath.

"Maybe the internal clock got reset when it got wet."

"Which was your fault," I said, taking the computer back.

"But it doesn't have any effect on the readings. If that's the worst outcome, then I think we got off pretty lightly."

We? We? This is all down to him. He was the one that jeopardized the whole project. He's the one who hasn't an ounce of professionalism in him. I was on the verge of telling him what I thought. Fuck the other guests. Then the hotel manager came out, and just stood watching us.

"This isn't over," I said to Ewan, turning back to my room.

"It never is with you," he shouted after me. "It never is."

### Site Diary
### 21st October

It's unfortunate that I have to record that the research has come to an end. Due to administration problems we are no longer able to continue with the project at this time. It is the hope of all the project staff that we can return to finish off our research at a later date, but it is not felt that we able to proceed any further this season.

## Jenny Calburn's Personal Diary
### 21st October

It's over. The whole project is fried. The permits were in place, but no-one had actually spoken to the landowner. He was waiting for us when we arrived this morning, leaning on the gate. Claimed he'd never been asked for permission. Never even heard of MacSanders. Demanded we get all our equipment off site straight away.

Ewan tried to reason with him, with the subtlety of a flying brick. I went to help calm things down, but he held up his hand and waved me away. Fucking waved me away! I left him to it and went back to talk to the students who were unsettled. Mostly worried about their grades. I couldn't give them any answers. How could I? Instead I watched Ewan try and dampen the fire of the landowner's anger by throwing petrol on it. When the guy went back to his car and came back with a gun, I stepped in, dragged Ewan away and got the students back into the minibus. There was nothing worth recovering on the site. We hadn't unpacked the surveying equipment yet, so that was safe.

We still have a week before we fly back. I don't know what to do now.

I didn't feel like company so fired up the computer and started processing the surveying data, and putting it into the CAD programme.

Most of the points actually looked OK. The students had done a good job on the topographic survey, and at least there are concrete results there they can be graded on. Something odd though. That cluster of anomalous readings prefixed by $\Theta$. Incredibly dense. When I overlaid them on the basemap, they're all around the tunnel. At first I thought they were some error from bringing in the benchmark but every single one is at the far end of the tunnel. Out of curiosity I opened the data log. They were all taken during that hour after midnight. One other thing. When I first spotted these odd readings in the data I counted three. Now there are forty eight. I don't know what Ewan did, but I think there might be some kind of virus in the programme.

### Site Diary
### 22nd October

As we still have three days until our flight back to England, we have decided to take advantage of our spare time, and use it for documentary research. The students have divided into groups and each group has been assigned a different archive to investigate.

While they're researching the project management team are processing the survey data.

### Jenny Calburn's Personal Diary
### 22nd October

I've refreshed the data several times and the problem just seems to be getting worse. Every time the number of points around the end of the tunnel increases. All with the same date stamp. I was reluctant to show them to Ewan. I knew he would blame me. He did. Accused me of corrupting the data. Accused me of introducing a virus. I could definitely smell the alcohol on his breath. Saw a three quarter empty bottle of bourbon by his bed.

We refreshed the data. Reloaded it into the CAD programme. There were more. Like a rash. All in the same place.

"Have you tried rotating the image?"

It seemed so obvious after he said it. Of course the third measurement the survey records is height. I dragged the cursor across the screen and tilted the image to see the heights of the points. They were still stacked upon each other, but rising. Ewan slammed the screen shut.

"I'm going to take this and see if I can sort out your mess."

I grabbed the laptop and he wrenched it from my arms.

"This is a university project and a university laptop. You're not working on this any longer."

What could I do? I'm not getting into a fist fight with him. I let him go. Let him take the computer. I'd got a backup of course, not that I had anything to open the files on.

### Jenny Calburn's Personal Diary
### 30th October

Because of events that happened on the 23rd I haven't had chance to write. With the police interviews and shepherding the students back home away from the press. The university has arranged counselling for us. I've declined so far, but don't know how much longer I can put it off. I want to get the project wrapped up.

That morning, some of the students had been concerned about Ewan when he didn't get up for breakfast. Honestly, by this point I didn't give a shit. They tried knocking on his door, but got no answer. Eventually they persuaded me to get the hotel manager to open up the room.

The smell hit me first. That iron tang of blood. The laptop was at one end of the bed, screen spidered and jagged. It took me a few moments to see Ewan fallen down the far side, duvet pulled down on top of him, only his fingers visible. What I remember, what will stay with me, is the splinters of computer screen glass wedged into his fingertips, clots around the wounds. That image, more than what he'd done to his eyes, is the one I wake up to in the middle of the night. That laptop glass piercing his skin.

And the laptop. I tried to get the police to let me take it, or at least copy the data off it. Not a chance. Lots of talk of evidence, and it being wrecked far beyond saving anyway.

There were too many things to sort out. All the students had to give evidence. Wasn't until we got home I remembered the back up.

I loaded it onto my desktop PC earlier, to check I had a full copy of the data. The least I can do is salvage the survey transects so the students can get their marks. When I loaded them into the programme the anomalies were there. I tried deleting them and refreshed the rendering. They increased, still in that spot on the far side of the tunnel, but something strange happened. Every time I ran the programme and tried to shift them, they increased in number. That was all at first. I rotated the view. They were higher each time. Then something changed again. There were no more, but the x,y coordinates changed. Each time I refresh the programme the concentration of points gets closer. I'm on the forty ninth iteration now. The points are still migrating. I've just looked away long enough to write up this diary entry, but I have to go back and check on what's happening. I'm not sure if I will be able to stop looking. I've just refreshed the data again. It's like there's a shadow in there. I'm not sure what will happen, but if you find this, the data is on the external drive. I don't know if we've made an error. If the equipment was defective or damaged. My eyes are stinging now. I've just refreshed again. The points are moving toward me. I need to stop writing now and just watch.

I've tried to track down some information on both Ewan and Jenny, but there's not much out there. I don't know if Ewan is a first name or surname, so that's a dead end. I did find a couple of mentions of a Jenny Calburn who wrote an MA thesis looking at navvy camps. Everything seems to end in the mid 2000s, and though I called in some favours I can't find any other papers by her. I even checked the archaeology magazines for obits. She just seems to disappear.

Steve Toase

Tuppence
a Bag

The toxic avian archaeology below Zoe's feet was not her concern. A stratigraphy of dead birds, bone-bare and time-plucked, were of no interest to her, despite the depth of time marked in dishevelled feathers and piles of shit.

Her job was to catalogue the factory's architectural features, the old ironwork and the windowed office set up to allow the managers all those years ago to constantly observe their workers. To photograph the game boards scratched into floors and triangles of cigarette butts in hidden corners.

Sweat ran down the neck of her chemsuit. She positioned the tripod and adjusted the camera, letting the light meter settle. Changing her footing, hollow bones popped beneath her boot and she winced.

Footsteps echoed from above where Maggie was recording the upper floor of the building. They'd been working together for a couple of years, mostly alongside each other, but the factory was vast and the Historic Building Survey had a strict deadline, one not made easier by the state of the place.

Time had made the building treacherous. Metal had been stolen by the desperate, industrial waste fly-tipped by the careless. Over everything lay a carpet of dead birds, dander, a fine powder from their rotting wings, dangerous enough to need protective equipment normally worn while tearing out asbestos.

Making a record in her notebook, Zoe picked up the camera and tripod, moving them a couple of metres to photograph an original door which had survived the factory's long afterlife pretty much intact.

Above her the dead birds' descendants called to each other, unaffected by the human intruders in their kingdom. How many bird generations had been born and died since the building was abandoned. Five? Fifty? She noted down the photographs and moved the camera once more to record some 1950s worker graffiti.

The cooing reminded her of cold Saturday mornings waiting at her grandad's pigeon loft for his birds to come into view, crest the roofs of the estate and come to rest.

When the old man died no one bothered to check on the birds. None of her relatives cared. She was away at university at the time. By the time of the funeral, all his champions had starved. She buried the small frail corpses in the woods where her grandad always took his dead birds.

Some of the family wanted to burn them or leave them out for the foxes. No way her grandad would have put up with that. The feathers brushed against her hands as she placed them in shallow holes and covered them back up with soil, bands still in place on their ankles. None of the factory birds had numbers, feral and free to live on crumbling window sills and die in vast burial mounds of their own creation.

"Zoe, can you come up for a moment?" Maggie's voice was loud and muffled. Several birds took to the wing at the disturbance, feathers strobing sunlight as they changed perch. Zoe reached into her site bag for a small handful of seeds, casting them against the wall. They hit, scattering, ready for the pigeons above to find later. They might be ragged but they still deserved to eat.

Turning off the camera, Zoe crossed the bone-littered floor. Flakes of dried pigeon skin in the air swirled away from her. Checking the strength of each stair before committing, she made her way to the floor above.

Maggie stood leaning against the wall, mask hanging from her neck and a cigarette hanging from her lips. She pointed to the far end of the room and nodded.

"I've no idea how they got up here, but I need to move them so I can get some clear shots of the wall."

Several barrels had been stacked under the eaves, any safety labels long faded and rotted as the metal itself became corroded by time.

Zoe walked across for a closer look. Over the years the seams around several of the lids had separated, becoming crusted with white yellow foam.

"They look pretty far gone," Zoe said.

"Still need to move them," Maggie said, crushing her cigarette out against the stone wall and dropping the filter into a small metal tin. There was no question that they would do it. The chain of command might be small, but it was still there. Maggie was the Historic Building Surveyor for the Archaeology Unit and Zoe was her assistant.

Nominally it was a training position. The main lessons over the past few months had been that old buildings are as dangerous for what's in them as what state they're in, and Maggie had a very loose relationship with health and safety. But it meant Zoe had a job when the usual archaeology site work came to an end, and she was mostly inside during the winter months, even if she was encased in a paper suit that meant she sweated twice as much as usual.

Maggie repositioned her mask and slid her hands into a pair of old gardening gloves then nodded to the waiting barrels.

Standing either side they walked the first container across the room, then the second. The third was a little heavier, but finally moved and they stacked it next to the first two.

"Only five more to go," Maggie said. Zoe gave her a thumbs up and was glad the mask hid her expression.

The fourth barrel did not move with gentle persuasion.

"Bit more force. After three," Maggie said. Zoe nodded and felt along the edge of the metal to get a better grip. "One. Two. Three."

Afterwards Zoe wasn't sure who had fucked up. With a wrench they pulled the barrel to one side. The weight inside shifted, sending it clattering to the wooden floor, impact tearing away the lid. Black tar-like liquid seeped out, pooling on the floor. Where the barrel had corroded to its neighbours its movement tore a hole in the others, now also leaking a black viscous liquid.

"Over here," Maggie said, standing by the stairs. The leak covered most of the floor and was starting to drop through the floorboards. Zoe stepped around until she was beside her boss, then followed her down.

Back on the factory floor, Maggie gestured toward the main entrance. Zoe followed, glancing behind. The substance was now dripping from the ceiling to rain black on the dead birds below, leaving a thin black sheen over feather and bone alike and pooling in empty eye sockets. The early afternoon sunlight reflected back and Zoe couldn't shake the feeling that the dead pigeons were looking at her.

Outside, they walked to the Land Rover, pulled back their hoods and took off their masks. Unlocking the door, Maggie reached in and turned on the radio, grabbed a pack of cigarettes, took one out, lit it and closed her eyes.

"I'm sorry Maggie," Zoe said.

"Not your fault," Maggie said, tapping ash on the floor. "You weren't to know that they were so corroded. That's on me."

"Still," Zoe said. "Sorry."

"Honestly, not your fault," Maggie said, taking a last drag. "Where did you leave the camera?"

"Downstairs on the left," Zoe said.

"I need to grab my kit. It's beside the bottom of the stairs and I'll get yours on the way out."

"I'll come in too."

"No need for both of us. You do some paperwork or something. I won't be long."

Zoe finished stripping off the paper suit and sat down in the passenger seat. Truth was there was no paperwork to do. Reaching for her site bag, she slid her hand past her tools for a small bag of snacks.

The radio was loud enough for her not to notice the noise at first. Even though the building was old, and the original owner powerful enough to not care about noise pollution, the walls were still good at muffling any activity within.

Zoe recognised the sound, the same as when a fox got near her grandad's pigeon loft; the sound of wing against wing and panicked birds flying into each other.

Climbing out, she finished eating, grabbed a fresh chemsuit and mask, and dragged them on over her clothes. Now the sound was worse, punctuated by percussive echoes against the stone walls.

Out in the sun the protective suit was far too hot and Zoe walked over to be in the shade of the factory. Close up, the sound was deafening. She pulled the mask into place and opened the door. Above her several birds flew out. She ignored their bid for freedom. It took a few seconds for her eyes to adjust to the darkness within the building.

The whole floor rippled, feathers and bone straining against layers of droppings. Even through the mask she smelt the acrid burn of disturbed decades old piles of shit.

The whole mass of dead birds was covered in black sludge. Several cavities had been torn through the mound of the dead. She glanced up. The air was thick with dove dust, swirling in the shadows, and above the dust the pigeons themselves.

Some were feral birds, descendants of the dead. Those looked ragged enough, torn and beaten by the ravages of city scavenging. There were other pigeons on the wing above her far worse.

Even from a distance she saw feathers missing from their tails, heads bare bone, empty eye sockets staring from above broken beaks. Some had no plumage at all, strands of muscle dangling from yellowed skeletons. Zoe became so transfixed by how they were staying aloft that she did not notice the screaming until it was too loud to ignore.

Zoe barely made out the figure of Maggie lying at the bottom of the stairs. Starting to run, she ignored the sound of her work boots cracking hollow bones.

Up close she saw the reason Maggie was so hard to recognise. Her boss was covered in dead pigeons. From head to toe they clung to her, claws slicing through her paper suit, now blossoming with blood. Several pigeons had tangled skinless legs in her hair and were scraping their beaks through her forehead to the bone beneath. Another had buried its head in her eye socket, scraping around inside. Maggie's arm lay stretched out to one side. A single bird nested in her hand as if waiting for its brood to emerge. The lack of feathers and muscle meant any chance of raising fledglings was a distant memory. The dead pigeons looked up at Zoe's approach.

She had no plan. Shoo them away? Give first aid? Drag Maggie toward the exit and hope the flock took flight?

They stared at her getting closer. A black tar-like substance seeped out of hollow bones.

The pigeons did not move. These were no longer fretful creatures begging crumbs below city benches. Already dead, the pigeons had nothing left to fear. Certainly not from her.

The door was a straight run behind her. Even walking she could reach it before the birds could reach her. There was nothing she could do for Maggie except recover her corpse at another time. That wouldn't happen unless she got out of the factory and raised the alarm. Grinding her foot into the decades thick layer of bones, feathers and bird shit, she readied herself to run.

The ground shifted below her. Zoe barely managed to keep upright. Between where she stood and the door, the whole floor was moving, rippling. Piece by bird shaped piece, the floor rose into the air.

Some of the corpses were skeletal, held together by the stretch of dried tendons, some caked with a gritty residue and the feathers of other dead pigeons. Close by her feet, two pigeons welded together by death crawled up from under a pile of rotten wood. By the wall several mummified squabs clung to the stone.

The air was thick with the dead. Every few seconds more and more dragged themselves free of the burial mound, cutting off her escape.

The manager's office was raised off the ground and sealed. None of the pigeons had managed to colonise it. Not looking back, she ran to her side, stamped across resurrected corpses, feeling them shatter with every footstep, the flock of those who could fly growing with every moment.

She felt them in the air behind her, wings spraying her with flaked skin. Reaching the steps up to the manager's office, something gripped the back of her chemsuit and she flinched, reaching back to brush it off. Another pecked through her glove, trying to clamp the tendons in the back of her fingers. Screaming, she flung it away to one side, watching the already dead pigeon land on the factory floor, climb to its feet and take flight once more.

The office door opened inwards. Zoe ran inside and slammed it shut behind her. Two pigeons clung to her suit, tearing holes with their beaks, trying to get at the warm meat below. As fast as she dared, she grabbed them, opened the door a little and threw both back into the factory.

The pigeons kept coming.

Zoe walked around the hexagonal room, staring out in one direction after another. The flock was concentrated on one side, wave after wave battering themselves against the windows, succeeding in doing nothing apart from smearing the glass. Between the feathers she saw Maggie's body on the floor. Several pigeons had returned to the paper suited corpse and were tearing through damp muscle to the white glistening bone beneath.

Designed for insidious surveillance of workers by management, the 360 degree visibility gave Zoe a chance to weigh up her options. If only the resurrected dead would stop flying at the windows, then there might be a chance to concentrate and plan a way out. There was no way for them to shatter through the reinforcement; the factory bosses all those years ago were too concerned about tools 'accidentally' slipping out of hands to use normal glass.

From above a new sound joined the cacophony of feathers and bones, a sound that took her straight back to her grandad's pigeon loft.

A pigeon in distress was the worst sound in the world. Most died quickly, either by bullet, jaws or a quick twist of the neck when they were beyond saving, but a bird dying slowly? They made sure the whole world knew.

She saw them, the already dead mobbing the still living. Dragging the victims to the factory floor, they pinned them in place to the concrete, and plucked out the tiny hearts. Slowly but surely they dripped the black chemicals into the chest cavity, feathers bowing out with the pressure.

One by one they slaughtered them all, until no living birds remained in the factory. Some tried to flee for the gaps they used to venture into town and scavenge, but the corpse pigeons knew and were there first, bringing the frightened creatures down with sheer weight, five or six hanging off each wing. Soon there were no living or dead, just the recent dead and the ancient dead.

Around the office the corpses never stopped flying, until the newly murdered pigeons were ready to take flight, then the flock settled to the factory floor. One by one the plump feathered birds rose away from their killers. They weren't elegant, as if they only half remembered how to fly. Sunlight came through shattered tiles and glistened off the black chemicals coating their eyes.

They came to rest on the office roof. She saw their tail feathers hanging over the edge, fringing the office. One by one they emptied their bowels.

Droppings streaked down the glass, smearing and coagulating until Zoe could no longer see outside, glass beginning to steam and melt. On every side the recently dead defecated down the windows, their chemically enhanced shit weakening the barrier.

Unsure of what to do, Zoe stood in the middle of the room and watched the glass thin. The flock took to the wing once more and rotting bird after rotting bird careered into the windows, pulling away melted glass fused to bare bone.

Inside the office Zoe looked for somewhere to shelter. The room had long been stripped of any furnishings. The roosting pigeons above still emptied themselves while their ancestors flung themselves again and again at the weakened windows.

It took a moment for Zoe to notice that all their efforts were concentrated on the five main windows, the narrow frosted glass in the door making her almost invisible to the birds beyond.

Quiet and slow, she unlatched the door and glanced outside, trying to estimate the distance to the main entrance. Now all the pigeons were trying to break the glass, maybe they were distracted enough with the task to let her escape. Maybe they were too focussed on the office to notice her.

More and more corrosive bird droppings dripped down the windows, bones separated from wings and ribcages staying in place. The flock might catch her before she got out. She might fall down the stairs and be feasted upon like Maggie. One thing was for sure though – if she stayed where she was it was only a matter of time before they got through. She needed to prepare.

First she stripped her chemsuit down to her waist, took off her jumper and put the protective clothing back on. Never taking her eye off the dead birds she wrapped the jumper around her head, then placed her hand on the door handle and waited. There was a rhythm to their attacks, their waves, like they were thinking with one intent. Hive mind. She waited. On the far side the glass began to crack. She waited. The first bird got its beak inside. She waited. The hole was big enough for the creature to get in, losing the last of its feathers on the way. Zoe opened the door and ran.

The flock was so focussed on getting into the office they did not notice she was no longer there until she was almost at the exit. She risked a look over her shoulder. Most were trapped, flapping around the office trying to kill someone no longer there. When they realised their victim had fled, the sheer crush of them all trying to leave at once sent many to the floor, too broken to be able to take to the wing. Enough escaped though, soon joined by the still-feathered recently living.

Reaching the entrance, she wrenched open the door, not caring about splinters tearing up her hands, and ran to the Land Rover, shutting herself inside. She rested her head against the dash and waited for her breathing to settle before taking off her mask.

Outside was a bright summer's day. The park across from the factory was packed with people finishing work early and making the best of the weather. Some were feeding ducks in the small lake and Zoe saw grey feathers in the trees. She turned back to look at the factory. The roof was the same grey.

Hundreds of pigeons crowded the gutter. Some had been dead for decades, in the daylight she saw how truly ragged they were, others killed and resurrected only moments before. Black streaks blistered the stonework.

More and more gathered, squeezing out of gaps under the eaves, through broken tiles and through the entrance that, in her rush to escape, she had not shut properly behind her.

One by one they took to the wing, darkening the sky as they flew across to the park, streaks of shit corroding metal railings and tarmac alike. Several emptied their bowels onto the 4x4's roof and she listened to the paint bubbling.

The pigeons did not attack the people. First they took to the trees, taking down the other pigeons they found. In the middle of family picnics and keep fit sessions they pinned the living birds to the grass and transformed them into living corpses like themselves. The screaming started off as disgust but soon turned to terror.

The pigeons mobbed the people one by one. Some were torn apart by precise beaks, others blinded as birds emptied their bowels of the toxic sludge. At least one was choked to death as bird after bird forced their way into his open mouth, stretching their victim's throat as they reached his stomach and pecked their way out from the inside.

Zoe watched some people try to escape, only to be pushed to the ground by the weight of wings. In the street between the factory and the park drivers abandoned their cars, unsure of where to run. The flock picked them off one by one.

Above the streets, the air darkened with oil coloured feathers as fragments of the flock took to the air once more. Zoe watched them assemble into a swirling mass, then split once more as they spotted new targets. Several smears of bird droppings hit the windscreen and, almost lazily, the glass turned liquid and thinned. Staying still would not save her. The only chance of survival was to leave.

Trying to still the shake in her hand, Zoe started the ignition. On the other side of the fence, a family lay choking on the pavement, mouths clogged with thick grey dust.

She dared not get out to open the site fencing. Instead, she drove at the gap, pushing the panels apart with the vehicle, dragging the hollow rubber boot holding the panels until the wire buckled and fell, leaving a gap big enough to drive through. Everywhere pigeons feasted on the crowds.

Bodies lay across the road and pavement, outlines distorted by fluttering wings, some feathered and some bare bones. Zoe knew there was no saving the fallen. She closed her eyes, took a breath and drove over the obstructions, turning up the radio to drown out the sounds of bodies, both small and large, splitting under the weight of the vehicle.

Beyond the park, beyond the factory, beyond the streets that surrounded them, everything felt normal. There was no panic, no sense of what was coming, the only sign was emergency vehicles streaming in the opposite direction. Zoe glanced in the rear view mirror. Beyond the blue lights, the sky was black with birds looking for their next victims, and the next birds to increase the flock.

The breeze was starting to pick up the cloud of dried skin now, swirling it past the factory and park. She watched it drift across people and cars alike, falling like Saharan sand. The coughing was delayed. Soon pedestrians began falling to their knees gasping for breath.

Traffic mounted the kerb to let police and ambulances through. Zoe took her chance and drove through the gaps. On the radio the music finished, leaving vague news reports of some kind of attack. Eye witnesses did not describe an explosion, just a thrumming sound and a grey powder. How do you describe the sound of thousands of dead pigeons taking to the sky? People stumbled out of the immediate area covered in scratches and burns, unable to describe what happened. Zoe carried on driving. Soon everyone would have the same idea.

The screams were getting louder, closer. She risked another glance behind. The grey mass in the sky was larger, glimpses of red on beaks and the white of bone. There was one place she could go to get away from the stench of blood and muscle and bird shit that was following her through the streets.

Time had taken its toll on the pigeon loft, wooden panels rotted and long since split. Chicken wire hung down in lazy curls as if the whole structure was some kind of overripe fruit. Above her the sky was clear. In the distance the flock was expanding over the town as they found more birds to resurrect. She wondered how long it would be until they found the corpses so carefully buried in the woods, pecked away the soil and gifted them the half-life of the undead. She wondered how long until her grandad's champions returned to the skies, until they remembered the homes they left so long ago. She would wait there until they returned. She owed her grandad that much. Across the city the sky was a mass of feathers, the buildings below covered in fine dust, the streets in corpses. Not long until they found their way back home. Not long at all.

# Breach!

With soil-stained hands and muttered words on his breath, the Lutumancer crawled across the topsoil-stripped site on his hands and knees, laying out protections that would keep the archaeologists safe during the excavation.

First he entwined the fifty two archaeological herbs around the boundary of the derelict building plot, to honour the whole of time. From a skin bag at his throat, he took out a small human figure made of the three sacred colours of clay, shattering the effigy upon the scraped back soil below the location of their excavation. Next he soaked the ground with a libation of rainwater and nettlewine, the limbs of the figurine melting back to mud in the torrent.

Site director Madeleine Slofelder watched him from the site office window, still transfixed by the pre-excavation rituals, even though she had seen them thousands of times before. From the floor, the Lutumancer picked up handfuls of gravel, scattering stone and grit to still the air, each grain of dirt spinning like a tiny planet scoured of life.

She picked up the site diary, walking down the metal steps and across to where the Lutumancer continued to murmur, flinching only slightly as the suspended spoil brushed against her skin.

"Are we ready to start?" she said, looking around at the preparations. Technically he outranked her, but this was her excavation, and he would follow instructions. The Royal Charter insisted on such a chain of command.

"The area is proscribed following the plans provided."

She nodded and opened her bag, taking out red and white silk ribbons to mark the trenches. Pacing out the edges in broad strides, she placed a skein at each corner. When she spoke the survey words of command, the ancient angular syllables scratched her throat raw. She paused to take a sip of water, stepping back as the ribbons unfurled vertically, precisely defining the limits of their excavation. Their tools would not work outside the provision given by royal assent. The air inside was paused and held. Not moving. A necessary step to allow them to peel away the layers of time. Stillness filled her thoughts. This was the moment of being an archaeologist she loved best. The anticipation of what would be uncovered as they scraped away the years. As they revealed the past. The first to see some of these events for two thousand years. She took a deep breath. Paused air always tasted sweeter.

"Meeting," she said to no-one in particular. "Site office."

Though the room was temporary it was well appointed. A desk at the back was spread with files to record layers and finds uncovered, the master site plan on the wall. In the centre was a large trestle table around which the whole team now sat. Madeleine took her place and clasped her hands.

"As some of you will know there has been no evaluation phase for this project. Instead we are responding to local information that made its way back to the Palace which, under the terms of the Royal Commission, required the Archaeological League to schedule emergency excavation.

"Ellie, can you take us through the evidence so far? Branwen, can you then give us the health and safety briefing?"

Ellie stood, straightened her overalls and pointed to an illustration pinned to the wall. Muttered words spilt from her mouth, glittered the paper and became a blaze of blue along the ink lines as the drawing detached itself from the vellum.

"The butcher described a ghost, which is not unusual in itself. The communities in this part of the kingdom are notorious for their superstition."

Around the table her colleagues nodded. Madeleine shuddered at the memory of the house gutter paintings the area was known for.

Fates the owners wanted to reflect back out into the world. They were extremely graphic, bodies torn apart with muscles and tendons rendered in detail one would expect from those who had seen too much death.

"However it was the specificity, and the complexity of the description. Firstly they described the ghost as being coated in fabric that glowed red around the edges which suggests something has passed through the area and churned up time."

"It's pressing against the membrane," Madeleine interrupted.

"Exactly," Ellie continued. "Secondly, it was the description of the appearance."

She turned to the drawing once more, and repeated the incantation to compel the drawing to the centre of the table. As her voice increased in volume, so did the image.

"You will all notice the banner."

Madeleine watched the rest of them take in what they were looking at. The curled chain of the Revolutionary Squatters, the metal tags visible even in the memory sketch taken from the witness.

"The charms of your Royal Commission will protect you while working here. I do not need to explain to you what happens if the Common Wealth Chain starts being replicated. What the reaction will be from the Royal Office of Subject Behaviour."

"And the witness?" Ellie and Madeleine looked across at the speaker. One of the Guards.

"His children are now managing the family business," Madeleine said. There was nothing more to say.

Ellie sat back down and slowly the figure became pale and faded once more as it was withdrawn back into the ink.

Branwen took them through the safety briefing, describing the need to keep tools sharp. How not to carry fragments of time out of the designated spoil area. How to make sure the time excavated was carefully sorted into discrete piles allowing easy reinstatement of the site. How no-one should enter the excavation area outside work hours as there was no guarantee the protections would be in place. When finished she sat down and they all looked at Madeleine, waiting for her to speak.

"For the rest of the day I want you all to go to the tool store and make sure all the tools are sharp and the blade enchantments are in place."

"We're not starting today?"

Callum spread his fingers open and shut against the table as he spoke.

"We are," Madeleine said. "We are starting by making sure the edges of all the tools are keen enough to allow us to do our job properly. Don't worry. I'll be doing exactly the same. There's no rank or favouritism here."

The tool hut was small and cramped with all of them sat inside. Branwen placed the charms box in the middle of the floor and opened the lid. Each piece of magic appeared as a bunch of herbs, though faint and transparent. Part in one world and in another.

Madeleine hefted a mattock from the corner, laid it across her lap and held the charm in her right hand. Even though it was little more than words spoken earlier in darkened rooms, she felt the veined skin of vague flowers. Non-present yet very real. She smeared them across the metal blade, watching the rusted steel shimmer as the charm gnawed away at the corrosion. Once the steel shone, the magic began to slide into the metal. This was the tricky bit. Getting the enchantment to fix to the edge. Quickly she started repeating the Fixer invocation, getting faster and faster, feeding the spell more magic.

Madeleine had not worked with this team before. They had come to the Royal Commission as privateers, and she knew they were watching her. Waiting to see whether she really had the skills to lead such a delicate project. She had nothing to prove and did not give a shit about their opinions of her. She was in charge and knew that was how things needed to be.

To her right Callum was struggling to get the charm to fix. Already the petals were seeping blue light across his fingers, tendrils knotting under his skin.

Sighing, Madeleine put her mattock to one side, and whispered the three sacred syllables of extraction to draw out the magic, ignoring his wincing as the charm left his flesh.

"These are high quality and take some careful manipulation. We don't hand dig here. The charm goes onto the blade. Not ourselves."

"It's a bit more complex than I'm used to," he said.

"I can tell." One handed, she lifted the mattock from him and, loud enough for him to hear, fixed the magic in place. "These are fragile. You need to clearly enunciate every single symbol, otherwise the strands do not attach to the right material. You try." She passed him a spade, and watched as he took out another charm, spoke the words clear and precise, allowing the magic to settle in place.

"Better," she said.

Lighting her cigarette, Madeleine leant against the hut and stared at the red and white ribbons buffeting in the breeze.

"You didn't have to embarrass him like that."

It was one of the Royal Guards. The younger one, who always kept his hand on his sword as if it would fly out of its scabbard at any moment.

"I didn't embarrass him. I have more experience and helped him. That's what we should do with experience. Share it. If I let him into the site with half the charm embedded in his skin and the other half on the mattock blade... have you ever seen that happen?"

The Guard shook his head. She held out the lighter and waited while his cigarette flared to life.

"The charm allows the blade to enter through the layers of time. With only half the charm it cannot extract itself. The pressure of time can shatter the metal. Imagine what it can do to flesh and bone."

~

"I want two trenches to start with," Madeleine said, driving her trowel into the damp morning and dragging it down until it touched the dew covered ground, leaving behind a shallow scratch in the air. She continued until the scratch became a rectangle and a rough shatter of time clung to the trowel blade. With a flick of the wrist she shook it off.

"The first one here, and the second one on the far side. I'll work with Branwen and Callum. You other two take the second trench. Dig away the overburden and see if you can define any features."

Removing the present was donkey work. A job involving heavy lifting and observation. Watching for the interface where time changed. A skill that relied as much on sense of smell as texture. Madeleine bucketed away the spoil of accumulated present, pouring it onto the spoilheap, stopping only to check on the second trench.

"I think you're almost there. Good progress," she said to Ellie and Jim.

She glanced back toward the cluster of huts, the Royal Guards sitting on camp chairs looking bored. She never knew whether the Commission assigned them as prison guards or protection.

"Do you want me to send them away. Far away." The Lutumancer spun pebbles in the air above his palm. "I could drag them through the earth to the sea floor, or maybe to the heart of a solid granite plug."

She took a step away from his soil smeared robes.

"I don't think that will be necessary. They're just doing their job. I'm not sure what their job is, but they're not bothering me."

"As long as you're sure."

"We've got something." Callum stood back from the trench leaning on his mattock, blade scorching the grass.

"I need to check this," Madeleine said to the Lutumancer, trying to sound apologetic.

"Until later," he said.

~

The air smelt of burnt cinnamon and woodsmoke. Madeleine leaned into the trench and felt the slight press of resistance. There was a faint glimmer of something just beyond the membrane.

"Well spotted. Clean up, plan the features, take any measurements you can, then draw the past layers forward."

Branwen nodded. "Do you want us to take samples?"

Madeleine smiled and held out the small snap neck bags.

"One litre please. Bag up some of the overburden so we can have it analysed for intrusions and residual finds."

The Lutumancer leant over Madeleine, his long hair brushing across her neck. She turned, stared and stepped out of the way.

"If I may," he said.

Madeleine gestured toward the scrapings of present day, giving permission but no blessing. He leant forward and pinched a fragment of time away from the spoil, extended his hair-covered tongue and let the grains settle, then swallowed. Madeleine waited for him to speak, but he said nothing.

Once the samples were taken, Madeleine pressed fragile wires into the exposed moments, waiting while the precise netting settled in place, then took up the drawing board and planned the shimmers just visible in the air.

When finished she beckoned over Branwen and Callum.

"Remember we're recording single context. Define the points of intrusion, plan the form. It looks like we've just got traces of the butcher on the site at the moment. Don't spend too much time, but I would like it recorded. Plans and context sheets."

"Madeleine."

She looked over at the second trench.

"We have something here too."

Before she approached the trench she felt how the layers of time were thinner. The area smelt of sea salt and charcoal. Once the overburden of the present had been stripped back the distant past was exposed, fragile and threadbare but there.

"Record what you have. Strip back to the feature, but carefully. We may need to lift this and take it back to the Royal Commission for further study."

She should have gone back to the first trench. Worked alongside Branwen and Callum as they dug their way through the paused layers of time, but she could not leave the discovery. The shimmering shuddering figure that stood in the trench.

Ellie pointed to the blurred feet of the figure.

"That looks far too old to be this close to the surface."

Madeleine reached out with her trowel and stilled the motion.

"Yep, those are at least four hundred years earlier than I would expect."

The Royal Guard was not aggressive as he moved her out of the way, though the way he did so gave her no opportunity to resist. Once he had cleared a line of sight he squinted at the shimmer of time in the vertical trench, looked from Ellie to Madeleine and peered back at the in-progress excavation.

"How can you make out anything?"

"Practice," Ellie said, shifting him to one side.

"Experience," Madeleine said, walking him away from the trench.

She looked at the litter strewn ground, then back up at him. He was young. Too young to wear so many scars.

"Why are you and your colleague here?" She spoke calm and even. Not because he had a weapon, or in fear of angering him, though both thoughts had crossed her mind. Because whatever the reason for his presence, it was not down to him.

"To keep you safe. Make sure no-one interrupts your work."

She pointed to the Lutumancer who knelt in a corner of the empty building plot, dissecting a dead rat with a shatter of brick.

"The charms he placed around us were not only to hook time in place while we worked. They're also to protect us. Believe me, a good Lutumancer who can call up the natural rock of the land to crush his enemies is far more effective than a couple of spearhands."

The Royal Guard could not look her in the eye, constantly glancing across to the chair where his colleague sat drinking lukewarm tea and smoking something banned in three provinces of the Kingdom, including the one they were in.

"You don't need his approval, do you?" she said, turning him by his shoulder. "I'm the site director. I can help you. Let you know if we find what you're looking for."

He nodded as he convinced himself.

"We're here to make sure nothing disruptive comes through from your work."

Madeleine did not smile, because that would be expected. Instead she turned him toward where the other archaeologists were busy recording intrusions and settlements of time suspended between the fluttering red and white ribbons.

"Nothing will be excavated that is disruptive to the Kingdom. No symbols of forgotten rebels. No subversive text. The past does not reveal itself in that way."

For a long time after, that simple sentence stayed with her as the moment in her life when she told the biggest lie.

Ellie stood in front of Madeleine, drawing board against her leg, not frowning or smiling. An expression of uncertainty as if she was unsure whether to interrupt.

"What is it?" Madeleine said, the issue with the Guard settled, whether he believed so or not.

"The figure you asked us to define and record. Something is pressing from behind. Something large enough to deform the time we're working on."

~

There was no argument. Ellie was correct. The figure closest to them was bowing out with pressure. Undulating as that pressure increased.

"Have you finished recording?" Madeleine said.

Ellie nodded and stepped back. Madeleine took her trowel from her back pocket, the worn handle sitting perfectly in her hand. She let the blade find the figure's edge and chased it, speaking a suspension charm to keep fragments of fill from scattering across the ground. Behind, time was compressed into lenses, little more than smears. Hundreds of them. Moments trapped between the bowed figure and whatever was coming from the past.

She felt the other archaeologists watching her. Waiting for her knowledge to manifest as instructions. Waiting for her to explain when she last saw something like this. Explain what they needed to do.

She let her experience manifest as confidence.

"There's too much risk of losing those lenses during excavation, and if the intrusion is dynamic, which it appears to be, then we might not have time. Lutumancer?"

He looked up, fingers smeared with moss and fur.

"Can you set each of these contexts with soil? Then we'll lift them and examine them in the site hut rather than in situ. Can you be precise enough?"

He smiled and picked up the remains of the rat. "I'm going to need more than one of these," he said. "Fresh, if possible."

~

The sound of ribs cracking accompanied every rise of sodden dirt from below their feet. She watched the Lutumancer smear them into place, then wait as Ellie and Branwen slowly peeled each layer away, carrying it into the site hut and placing it on the table.

Each one was barely there. If Madeleine crouched down to see them from the side they became invisible. She tied her hair out of the way and walked to the trench. The ground beneath was covered in divots where the Lutumancer's charms called forth soil to fix and strip each context.

They were no closer to the intrusion bulging out through time. No closer to reaching the source of the distortion. Each time the Lutumancer fixed a layer, another one emerged underneath, stretched and deformed. Madeleine, Ellie and Branwen busied themselves filling in context sheets, sketching the layers of time and taking samples. Recovering as much as they could from the paper thin remains, each one barely substantial enough to hold itself together. By the time the sun was setting behind the buildings, tiredness was leading to mistakes and they were no nearer to reaching the intrusion.

~

"You could just take a section. Go right through whatever is wanting to be reborn."

The Lutumancer stood next to Madeleine. She could taste the exhaustion coming off him. The stench of weariness.

"Whatever is doing this I'm not willing to risk the overlying history just because of some aggressive anomaly."

The Lutumancer yawned and rubbed clay from his knuckles into his eyes. The sound of grit against his irises made Madeleine wince, despite herself.

"Have you thought about what the anomaly could be?"

"Not really," Madeleine lied. "What do you think?"

"You're interested in what I think?"

"Of course," she lied again.

"Have you ever excavated a detonation?"

"Once or twice. But this is too early. It's a long time before the Crown powder mills started production."

The Lutumancer laughed and Madeleine felt her skin crawl.

"You believe the only thing that can explode is powder? I would think someone of your supposed experience would not be so naive."

She kept her hands on the table and stared at the latest context to be lifted from the trench, a young family trapped as if in aspic watching something she would never see.

"I have excavated twenty seven historic explosions, both as the result of powder detonations and chemical accidents. In all those cases the form and the shape of the contexts were the same. They had a jagged profile which erupted through everything else, piercing forward and back in time. Piercing every event before and after. They had multiple points of intrusion, often with slight fragments of time sent through the trench. Moments disrupted as if hit by shrapnel. This is far too regular. If you don't believe me I can have the site reports called up from the vaults for you to study them yourself. And learn something."

The Lutumancer smiled, though it didn't reach his eyes.

"I defer to your obvious expertise in the destruction of the past," he said. "And now I need to rest and recoup my energies."

Madeleine stepped back as the soil under her feet shifted, the cocoon of dirt filling the Lutomancer's mouth first, then coating him from scalp to ankles, baking as if he generated kiln heat from within.

She did not sleep at all that night, rising every couple of hours to gaze out at the trench, visible only because of the ribbons fluttering at each corner. The only sign that anything was going on. Yet she knew that the anomaly was there, stretching and warping time as it tried to find a way through. Maybe it would be better to backfill now. Seal it up and leave it. But what then? Maybe it would tear through to the present. Leave the excavation a dead zone. Maybe it would drag the present back through the churn. It wasn't unheard of. If she concentrated she thought she saw the anomaly shimmer. Or maybe that was just her tiredness.

The contexts above the intrusion were barely holding together, so warped there seemed little sense in recovering them. Any relationships worn and disrupted. There was no value in recording them in detail any more.

Branwen ran her trowel over the surface, sparks rising from the blade.

"What do you want us to do?"

Madeleine could ask no-one. There was no time to send a messenger to the Royal Commission or Archaeological League, and even if there was, any admission of failure would see her position become even harder to hold.

"Director?"

"Strip it all back."

"All of it?"

"We'll work in teams. I want the intrusion exposed by this afternoon."

Branwen nodded. Madeleine picked up a mattock, sighed and began to strip the ruined contexts away.

The sound the tools made when they hit the exposed intrusion sounded like a xylophone. Pure and clear.

Each time they dragged away a layer, there were more, each one churned like plough soil. She needed to monitor what the excavation teams were doing, but also needed to pull her weight. This was not the time for site diaries or records. This was a time to work through the damage to get to what was below. She wiped her forehead, dropped her mattock and took out her trowel, letting it glint against the intrusion.

The words were faint at first, Madeleine only able to hear them when she pressed her ear against the shimmer, but there was no doubt what they were. She glanced over toward the two Royal Guards. All their attention was on a game of cards they were playing for future rations. She walked across to the Lutumancer's sleeping cocoon and tapped on the surface. The soil softened, turned to wet clay and slid over her work boots.

"Yes?" he said, clearing clods of topsoil from his eyes and dragging spit soaked roots from his mouth.

"I need you to distract them."

"Interfere with Servants of the Crown?"

"Create a disturbance down the street. Something convincing enough to draw the attention of Servants of the Crown."

"Aren't we all Servants of the Crown though? Just their service involves more gristle."

"My attention is already fully committed," Madeleine said, glancing back to the trench in a way she hoped made it obvious without more explanation.

"A few moments then," the Lutumancer said, laughing at his own joke.

Madeleine watched him walk across to the spoilheap, grab a handful of time from the day before, mix it with some animal bones and wormcasts then press the mixture through the site fence.

The shouting was convincing. The sort of noise that has no words. Just tone and violence. Madeleine watched the Royal Guards' instinct come into play. Watched them climb out of their seats, and watched them leave to chase dissent elsewhere. She waited until they left the boundaries of the site, walked across to the gate and slid the padlock in place. She could have asked another to do this, but she wanted to make sure no-one else was implicated in the treason.

The intrusion was not just the song. Not just those long lost words. The intrusion was also the passion and rage those words inspired. The anger of the people those lyrics dragged out of their homes into the street to guard barricades and fight on the cobbles.

"SITE," she shouted, her voice only just audible over the shifting rage the Lutumancer had conjured up outside the excavation. The digging staff gathered around her, resting their tools on the floor, shimmers of blue just visible in the dirt.

"When we breach the intrusion all twelve underworlds will break loose. You have a choice. Go to the site hut and you can legitimately claim you weren't involved. If you help us I can't guarantee your safety."

"What are we dealing with?" Branwen said.

"If you know then it's too late," Madeleine said. "But once we breach, the Royal Guards who so far have sat around like bookends will not be so friendly."

"If it helps, I'm on your side," the Lutumancer said. Madeleine nodded.

"That might not be enough, but it's a start."

Madeleine watched the looks that went between the diggers. The expressions searching for the first one to fold. The first one to back down. No-one moved.

"Are we ready to do this?" she said, checking their reactions as if they were archaeological contexts.

A murmur went around the circle. Nervous but not backing down.

~

"Ellie, your memory is perfect and you have some musical background?"

"Played in the village band as a kid. Can still carry a tune," Ellie said. They stood side by side staring at the shimmer of the past suspended between the fluttering silk ribbons. Madeleine nodded. The others waited behind, willing to do what was asked.

"Your job is to focus on the words. Catch the lyrics. If there is a tune I need you to get that too. These are phrases from a long time ago so catch them the best you can. Are we ready?"

Another murmur of agreement.

The Lutumancer was right. There were other explosions than powder. Sound and rage on their own could explode through time. Combined they created an intention and momentum that just kept on going.

No-one had ever found the location of the first rebellion, the only successful one, and inside Madeleine was at war with herself. The side that needed to breach this pocket of rage and unleash it once more on a suppressed Kingdom, and the professional side that saw the need to record the historical event before it was lost.

The Royal Office of Subject Behaviour would never let the history be known. Might as well be hung for trying to achieve something, Madeleine decided. She reached into her back pocket and drove the point of her trowel into the intrusion.

The song was clear and precise even as it was carried forward to them by ten thousand dead voices. There was no need for Ellie to focus on the words. They were simple in their rebellion. Catchy. Easy to repeat. Easy to spread. In moments the rest of the site staff were singing, their voices raised in dissent.

The intrusion passed over them like a wave, spreading into the streets, being picked up in the whistle of the street cleaner and the yell of the costermonger.

Madeleine walked across to the gate and peered through the fence. Already walls and roads were being ripped apart to be used as barricades and weapons, the song taken up by ten thousand living voices. None of the makeshift choir's great grandparents were born when the words were last heard on the Kingdom's streets.

Outside the boundaries of the excavation she saw a flash of red, the scarlet of the Royal Guard's uniforms, and for a moment she worried for their well being as representatives of the Kingdom's violence. The two Royal Guards came closer to the fence, and as they approached she heard the words on their lips. The song of rage and rebellion found fertile ground in the minds of the conscripted and she watched them take off their uniform colours, tying them to the fence before joining the barricades.

Taking one last glance back to the site still erupting the rage of the past, Madeleine raised her voice in song and opened the gates to join the gathered crowds.

# Horn and Hoof

"What is it?" said Mr French, peering down at Jim from under his hard hat.

Behind him a herd of highland cattle crowded against the wooden fence, more interested in the fresh grass of the verge than any archaeology. Jim wiped the blood from his skinned knuckles and pointed to the other side of the trench with his trowel.

"Here we've got a wall coming across at a right angle to the Roman road over there," he said, standing to point past French at the motorway 200 metres away.

Mr French nodded and kicked in some spoil with the toe of a new rigger boot. Jim watched the loose soil land across the area he had just cleaned for a photograph. He felt his back tense, but kept the words inside.

"So you've got an old wall. Place is crawling with them," Mr French said.

"I haven't finished. That wall returns over there and in the corner we have a series of steps going down, possibly another two metres. And this," Jim reached over to turn a large piece of dressed stone "seems to suggest a temple of some kind."

Mr French took off his hardhat and banged it against his leg, the heat of the day making his pinched glasses slide again. The cows, and their calves, scattered at the noise.

"So does this mean you're holding the job up again?"

*Well if you will go putting a new trading estate in the middle of one of the largest Roman settlements in the country*, Jim thought to himself. But he managed to stay professional.

"I'm not sure you realise the significance of this site. A temple needs to be excavated properly, not as an add on to a watching brief."

"I'm not sure you realise, Mr Archaeologist, that every time you delay like this you are costing us, and by us I mean the lowly tax payers of this district. The people I answer to. You don't live round here do you?" Mr French sighed and turned on his heel, knocking more dust over the trench.

Jim reached into his pocket and pulled out the site mobile. Wiping the grit and sun cream off his fingers he dialled, listening to the answerphone kick in.

"Hi Sam. More problems on site. Looks major this time. My guess is some kind of temple. I'll send you some photos tonight, but I'm going to have to stop the work until you can get out here.

Does the planning condition give you powers to stop the work? Ring me later."

Phone away he climbed out of the trench, leaning on the machine bucket to take some record shots.

Frank, the machine driver, walked over and grabbed his flask from the cab.

"Sorry Frank we can't dig anymore today."

Frank laughed and poured himself a cup of coffee.

"Doesn't bother me son. We went onto day rate as soon as you found those stones."

He reached into his pocket for a pouch of tobacco, rolling two, lighting them and passing one to Jim.

"So what are you scratting around with now?"

"Do you know Frank I'm not completely sure. Gut feeling is some kind of temple."

"You mean like sacrificing virgins? Not many round here these days."

Jim laughed as he picked up a tray of cattle bones and passed it across to Frank. "More likely animals. First guess would have been a temple to Mithras, but they didn't sacrifice animals as far as I can remember. Could be to a local god. Lot's of little cults around at the time. My Romano British archaeology is ok, but in fifteen years I've not seen anything quite like this. I need a second opinion really."

Frank started to speak. Jim cut in, "Unfortunately on this one it has to be from someone other than you."

Frank nodded across to the shiny new pool car, where Mr French sat scowling into his mobile phone. "You want to watch that little prick. Wouldn't trust him as far as I could spit." To clear his throat, or possibly show Jim how far this was, Frank spat into the spoil heap. "Not as far as I could spit."

~

It was raining. He could hear it battering down on the moor, on the stones, feel it on his skin. The blindfold felt coarse, chafing against the skin where he had recently shaved. Callused hands held his arms, leaving bruises. He could smell woodsmoke, sweat; his own fear. The steps felt uneven under his feet, and twice he lost balance, the figures invisible behind him stopping a broken nose or cracked skull.

The air changed. No longer the rain-stung wind, but stale and dry. Hands pushed him forward into the dust and dirt. He lay there, hands exploring the floor; the smooth stone of the walls. Then his world was filled with noise, unlike anything he had heard before. A bellowing filled his skull, driving away all thoughts, leaving an empty hollow space. Then the rain came, slowly at first, building into a torrent. He lay on the ground as rivulets ran off him, and he tasted the iron of wave after wave of blood, gluing sand and grit to his skin. The liquid stuck the blindfold to his face, dripped down his hair, into his open mouth, choking him. And still the deluge would not stop.

Jim woke wrapped in his bedding, sweating and breathing heavy from a panic that lingered long after the dream faded.

~

"What the fuck did you do Frank?"

Jim stood on the edge of the trench and looked down at the now destroyed stonework, the inscription rendered unreadable by three parallel machine gouges through the carving.

Frank looked at the ground, not meeting Jim's eye.

"I did what I was told, son. As always. I did what I was told."

Behind them a car pulled up. Jim carried on staring at the trench as the door opened, shut and footsteps walked up behind him.

"Morning gentlemen. How are we today?"

Frank looked over at Jim, raised his hands, stared at Bob French with a look of utter contempt then walked away to the site hut.

"Have you any idea what you've done, Mr French?" Jim carried on staring down at the wrecked site. He knew if he turned Bob French would be smiling, a sanctimonious crooked smile, and he knew restraint would go out of the window.

"Oh dear Jim. I'm sorry to see that. You know how enthusiastic some of these machine drivers can get. They do end up carried away sometimes."

"I spoke to Frank myself at the end of play yesterday. He knew to leave this alone."

"Not the brightest lads. That's why they're stuck on these machines rather than in a proper job," French said with a wheezing chuckle.

"A damn sight brighter than you Mr French, and a damn sight more fucking pleasant to work with. Get off my site."

"I think you'll find, boy, this is my site. We pay you. You work for us, not the other way round, and you'd do well to remember that."

Jim could feel his leg start to shake as his temper rose. He tapped his foot to feed away the adrenaline.

"You do know this is a contravention of your planning permission?"

Mr Frank smiled and rubbed his chin, "And the fine is what? £2000? £3000? The budget for this job is two million. I'm sure we can find it somewhere." He looked thoughtful for a second.

"I know Mr Archaeologist. I'll pay it with the money I've saved from not having to fund you to excavate some old remains."

He started to walk away, whistling, then stopped and turned back to Jim.

"And you can tell that girl from the Ministry about the unfortunate turn of events. Such a shame, but fortuitous don't you think?"

Jim ignored him and jumped back into the trench, lifting out tumbled stone, lying chaotic in the dirt. He ran his fingers across letters carved by minds dead for two thousand years and sat back on the tarmac, shoulders slumped, looking down at the drawing board by his side, all enthusiasm gone.

~

Sam followed him into the hut. He moved aside the lunchboxes and flasks, spreading out the drawings he managed to make before the walls were destroyed.

"I can't believe anyone would have the audacity to cause that much damage in a scheduled ancient monument," he said, sitting down at the table.

Sam flicked her now dead cigarette out into the scrub grass.

"I can. You need to be a little less naive Jim. There are characters like Mr French all over the shop." she said, sitting down next to him.

"You're not going to let him get away with it?"

"Of course not. Fucking hell Jim, how long have you known me? Of course I'm not. But with his money..." She shrugged, not needing to finish the sentence.

"So what will you do?" said Jim continuing to push.

"Well first of all I'll rip him a new arsehole. People like Bob French do not like being put in their place by a 5-foot-nothing female. All he'll do is offload the pain onto one of his staff who's fallen out of favour. Of course, he'll say, he understands why we need to pursue a prosecution, but Mr Scapegoat has a young family. He will of course be pursuing an internal disciplinary, but can we reconsider prosecuting Mr Scapegoat as he never meant any harm, and misunderstood his instructions. Mr Scapegoat will of course follow Bob French's guidance to the letter as jobs are hard to come by, what with the recession and 'You're not getting any younger' and 'I'd have to mention those times you came back to work after a couple of pints at lunch'."

Jim looked out of the hut to where Frank sat in his machine, flicking nervous glances toward the trench. It didn't take a genius to work out where that pain was going to land.

Jim pushed the drawings across the table to Sam, who flicked through them, then looked at the digital photos Jim had shot the previous day.

"For what it's worth Jim I think you're right. It is a temple, but not to Mithras. The inscription uses Latin conventions, but I don't recognise the name. I'll take these back to the office and run them by Simon River. He does most of our Roman sites for us."

She stood up and leant against the door-frame rolling another cigarette.

"Until I get back in touch the only person who goes anywhere near that hole is you, and you need to do everything you can to record what can be salvaged from this clusterfuck."

Jim's day brightened watching Sam talk down to Bob French. He'd seen Sam in action before, and to watch a short, slim blond girl put a truculent developer in his place always bought a smile to his face. He stood, drinking warm water, while Bob French stormed off, the screeching tyres as he drove away giving away the fury in his tight, pinched face.

Sam walked over.

"That went well," she said.

"So I see. Seemed to take it like a man," Jim said, burying his mattock in the spoil heap.

"If you mean a male chauvinist, never-been-talked-to-like-that-in-his-life man, then yes."

She jumped down next to Jim and reached in her back pocket for a trowel.

"Oi," said Jim "I thought I wasn't to let anyone else near this hole."

"I don't count. I'm like the north wind. I can go," she paused and twirled round, "anywhere."

Kneeling, she started to clean down the stonework he had freshly exposed. "You didn't think I was going to come out here, to a supposed temple, and not have a play myself. Honestly. Anyone would think you didn't know me. Oh and don't tell anyone at the office."

"Secret's safe with me," Jim said "You can shovel."

For the next half hour they worked next to each other, taking it in turns to dig down the spoil in the centre of the trench, shovelling onto the rapidly growing heap. Every so often

Jim shot a glance over at the JCB where Frank sat biting his nails and chain smoking. For the past week Frank had been the first to spot the archaeology in the trenches, stop the machine, lift out a little more spoil. Now he hung back like a scolded toddler.

"Jim. Have you seen this?"

He turned to where Sam was working. In front of her, surrounded by a small arc of loose soil, stood a flat dressed block of limestone. On the face hundreds of carvings of bull horns. Some large, others tiny, all shallow into the stone, overlapping, blurring the lines of the ones below.

~

That night Jim's dreams were filled with clay and blood, stones the size of dragon's eggs pressing against his open eyes. He woke to rain hitting the window in the dark, his wife still sleeping in calmer dreams.

~

"Health and safety. Couldn't leave it open. Someone might have had an accident. Wouldn't want that on your conscience would you," said Bob French, leaning against his car, the plan of works spread out on the roof.

Jim went over to the now filled in trench, walking across the type one aggregate that now left a white scar on the ground. He felt the rolled stone underfoot and could see the carvings in his mind's eye, now scratched and pounded by several tons of stone and a mini road roller. Inside he felt a rage that went far beyond professional concerns.

"Why? Why just go ahead and do this, French? Why not wait for me to get back to site? Or phone me? We could have covered the archaeology, put some sand in. Lifted the carvings."

Bob French smiled, his eyes squinting against the sun. "I tried ringing you, obviously. Must have been in an area without a signal. I'd change phone operator if I were you. And you might not realise it, I know you university educated types don't really live in the real world, but compensation culture being what it is I'm not going to let some unemployed no-hoper take council tax payers' money in some spurious injury claim. Nope, couldn't be left an hour later. Much too dangerous."

Jim tried phoning Sam, knowing that any action would now be symbolic, Bob French's arrogance making him untouchable. The little man standing up to pointless hold ups, in the name of the general public.

Jim walked over to the site hut, opening the door and sitting opposite Bob French across the table "So where does this leave us then?" Jim said, fingers knotted till the knuckles went white.

Bob French smiled, relaxed in his victory over another hold up.

"Well obviously we press on with the next stage of the project. I hope in an atmosphere of mutual respect, as much as I'd like you to go back to your ivory tower and leave us to do some proper work." He stood and walked to the door. "We'll be moving into that field next. I'm going to go and start laying out the trench, ready for the new machine driver on Monday. You can come and watch and make sure you are happy with the position. Wouldn't want to damage any of our shared heritage."

Jim got up and looked past him to the field.

"Aren't you going to wait until the farmer clears the field of livestock?"

Bob sighed. "City boy eh? They're only a few head of cattle. As long as you don't go near the young 'uns you'll be fine."

"Even so I think I'll stay this side of the fence. There's still paperwork to do."

"Suit yourself. No rest for the wicked."

Half an hour passed. Jim sat in the hut, context sheets and plans spread around. A simple matrix sketched on a sheet of paper, relating the different parts of the site to each other. Curiosity getting the better of him, Jim wandered across the site. Bob French crouched in the long grass, a trundle wheel stood beside him, his back to Jim. Jim stood on the lower rail of the fence and leant across to stroke the nearest cow. She turned and calmly nuzzled into his hand.

Afterwards he couldn't remember making the decision, or opening the knife he kept in his pocket for cutting string. The only memory that lingered afterwards was the smell of blood. The blood on his knife from where he stabbed it into the muscled flank of the cow, the blood on the thing that had once been Bob French now trampled by two hundred head of panicking cattle. The blood that flowed down from the squealing bull sacrificed above him in the dark.

Terminus
Post Quem

Daniel Benlainey BA MSc
Project Manager – Multivallate Archaeology
Unit 4 Sunray Farm
YK94 1SX
D.Benlainey@multivallate.org.uk

Simon Campbell BSc
Senior Archaeologist
Historic Environment Team
Callshire County Council
County Hall
Ostbarnton
YK56 4RF
Dear Simon,

Please find attached the interim site report for the Carrion Knoll Excavation. Hope everything is OK. We're still waiting on some results from a subcontractor, but I'll forward them as soon as they arrive.

Yours sincerely
Daniel Benlainey BA MSc

**Interim site report of Carrion Knoll Archaeological Excavations September 8th 2017**

Due to the position of the Carrion Knoll housing development in an area of known prehistoric and Roman activity, a planning condition for archaeological evaluation was required ahead of any groundworks.

Between August 1st and August 25th, a five-person team carried out the necessary work. Due to the low-lying nature of the site and anaerobic conditions found in certain areas, the quality of organic preservation was good, with several surprising results.

Three trenches, each 20m by 10m, were excavated. These were distributed across the development area to give as wide a spread of results as possible.

**Historic Background**

Carrion Knoll lies in an area of known Neolithic, Iron Age, Roman, and Anglo-Scandinavian activity, though no known archaeological material has previously been recovered from the exact site location. Since approximately 900AD, there is no evidence of activity in the vicinity.

**Trench 3**
**Context Record**

[01] Topsoil. A layer (average 0.4m thick) of black hummic sandy clay silt. Very little evidence of

recent agricultural activity. This layer covers the whole site, including all of Trench 3. The topsoil was removed by machine, and the spoil scanned by metal detector. Nothing of significance was found. The only finds recovered were eight clay pipe stems of various lengths and one incomplete clay pipe bowl, the incised decoration indicating a date somewhere in the early 19th century.

[02] Subsoil. A brown silty clay with regular inclusions of small rounded pebbles. This layer contained several residual pottery sherds of all periods, including a non-diagnostic fragment of Roman Nene Valley Colour Coated Ware, and five sherds of Iron Age Black Burnished Ware. All were heavily abraded.

[03] was assigned for the underlying natural geology, though this was not reached during the excavation due to the depth of archaeological deposits.

[04] A thick peaty organic layer only identified in Trench 3. This consisted of a firm dark green organic silt with a very high proportion of plant material, vegetation, and charcoal flecks. Occasional small angular limestone inclusions. This deposit covered all excavated archaeological features.

[05] Cut of large pit identified in Trench 3. This large feature had a steep edge with a base sloping to the centre and measured 1.2m deep and 2m in diameter. When excavated, this pit was found to have cut through an earlier deposit [11] and truncated a Samian bowl. Pit [05]

contained several fills. [06], [07], [08], and [09] seem to represent rapid backfilling of the pit. [10] is the primary fill.

[10] was the primary fill of pit [05] and was a friable dark grey organic silt with regular inclusions of vegetation. [10] also included several sherds of the Samian bowl identified in section and located in layer [11]. Whereas the ceramic remains in [11] are in very good condition (see below), the fragments recovered from pit fill [10] are not. The ceramic material has several bones accreted to it, which our osteological specialist (see Appendix Four) has identified as the phalanges from the hand of an adult human. In all cases, the bones press through the sherds and are visible on the other side. In places, the distinctive red slip covers the skeletal material. There is no evidence of burning on the bone, and as our ceramic specialist has pointed out (see Appendix Five), a vessel in such condition would not survive firing.

The ceramic sherds are clearly derived from the same vessel as that recovered from context [11] (see below), and date to sometime in the 2nd century AD. However, carbon 14 dating of the skeletal material has given a date of 850AD±25, which is contemporary with other finds from pit [05], including a broken antler comb (see Appendix Seven) and several well-preserved pieces of fabric (Appendix Eight).

[11] was a thick layer of dark grey organic silty clay extending across most of Trench 3,

into which the majority of the other features were cut, including pit [12] and graves [15] and [17]. The presence of a considerable number of Romano-British finds, including the Samian bowl truncated by pit [05] and several incomplete Nene Valley Colour Slip Ware vessels gives this a very secure *terminus post quem* of the 2nd century AD. The Samian vessel is discussed in more detail in Appendix Five, and the contents in Appendix Six.

The high level of organic preservation has led to the recovery of vegetable material, which has survived to such a degree that examination in the field allowed initial species identification, including hyssop, fennel, and wormwood. All were found in bunches tied together with some form of nettle string, and all had been placed in a circular arrangement around the Samian bowl. It must be assumed that when the vessel was truncated, any herbs placed on the western side were lost.

Cut [12] was a pit located in Trench 3, and to the west of pit [05]. In contrast to pit [05], pit [12] was very shallow in depth (150mm), just deep enough to take the contents. The edges were uneven, with several irregular shovel scoops at the base. Pit [12] contained a single fill [13].

[13] was a loose light grey silty sand with few inclusions. The majority of the pit fill was taken up by a single adult human skull (see Appendix Four).

[15] was recognised as a single isolated grave in Trench 3, cut into layer [11], with vertical

sides and rounded corners. This was clearly recognisable as a grave cut in plan, allowing careful excavation to enable the recovery of all human skeletal material.

[16] was the fill of grave [15]. The skeletal remains inside appeared to be of an adult human. The skull and phalanges of the left hand were absent.

Cut [17] was an additional grave identified further in Trench 3. The trench was widened by 2m to allow the full recovery of all skeletal material. The pit was 1m20 deep and contained fill [18].

[18] Very little soil matrix was recovered from fill [18], with most of the volume made up of butchered fragments of bone, including femurs, vertebrae, and ribs. A full discussion can be found in Appendix Four.

~

**Appendix Four**
**Human Skeletal Material**
**Report by Adrian Anchancy**
Several deposits of human skeletal material were recovered from Trench 3 of the Carrion Knoll excavation. Here I will go through them in context order and outline the physical evidence, followed by a discussion of the implication of the results.

[10] In an excavation where a large volume of skeletal material was recovered, the bones

found in fill [10] are unique. A group of five phalanges were identified, all of them cemented to sherds of Romano-British Samian pottery. This in itself is not unusual. Post deposition processes, such as iron panning, can lead to the accretion of finds in the ground. However, there are several aspects to the recovered bone that this researcher has not seen before.

The phalanges are not just concreted to the surface of the Samian ware, but actually pass through the pottery. There is no evidence of cracking to the clay or burning to the skeletal material. In at least one example, the characteristic red slip glaze coats the bone.

Having spoken to the ceramic specialist, Diane Bansetten, whose report can be seen in Appendix Five, the presence of such a large intrusion in the body of the vessel during firing would have led to destruction. In addition, exposing human bone to the high temperatures found in a Romano-British kiln would lead to severe discolouration and diagnostic cracking on the bone surface. Therefore, it is the opinion of both myself and my ceramics colleague that the bone must have been introduced post firing. Carbon 14 dating of the skeletal material has given a date of 850AD±25, which is not consistent with the age of the Samian pottery, suggesting it was introduced six to seven centuries later.

There are other issues with the condition of the phalanges. All show evidence of small holes in the outer surface of the bones. At first it was the opinion of this researcher that these were the pathology of some form of disease. On further examination, it was found that each lesion displayed evidence of microscopic tooth marks, consistent with certain types of immature coral larvae. When submitted to x-ray analysis, the tunnels can clearly be seen passing through the bone into the marrow. The sinuous form of the pathways also suggests that this damage was created by the actions of a living organism.

Tree root action was soon discounted, as there is no evidence for that type of activity within the contexts excavated or surrounding area.

[13] The skeletal remains from fill [13] (pit [12]) consisted of a single adult skull. It is not clear if the head was removed from the body pre- or post-mortem. There are several unusual features about the condition of the skull. The eye sockets show damage from a bladed weapon, particularly running from the infraorbital foramen into the supraorbital margin. On the right-hand side socket, there is clear damage to the lacrimal bone, and on the left-hand socket, repeated shallow strikes to inferior orbital fissure, reaching as far back as the sphenoid bone.

The position and nature of the damage allows us to discount any consideration of surgery. The physical evidence suggests that a blade has been repeatedly, and without control, forced into the eye socket. The result of this would be for the soft tissue of the eye to be completely destroyed.

None of the marks have been made to the edges of the eye-sockets, only to the upper and lower bones. The position and angle of the damage allows us to make some more inferences. It is the belief of this researcher that the damage was self inflicted. The size of the cuts suggests the injuries were made with a small eating knife common during the 9th century.

A second unusual feature of the skull is a series of lesions in the styloid process region. This displays similar characteristics to those seen in the phalanges recovered from fill [10], but the lesions are much larger in scale. Here the shape and form of the damage from gnawing is clearly visible to the naked eye, and suggests that the damage was created by a living organism.

[16] As noted above, the skeletal remains recovered from the fill of grave [15] were incomplete, lacking a skull and phalanges from the left hand. When compared to the skull and phalanges recovered elsewhere during the excavation, and discussed above, it is clear they are from the same individual.

The lesions observed in both previous skeletal finds are also evident here. One of the jobs that became essential post excavation was the mapping of the route these lesions took through the body. This was mainly achieved using x-ray analysis, which allowed the tunnels to be recorded. The preliminary results are published below. It became clear that whatever created the voids within the skeletal material also travelled through the soft tissue, and as it progressed through the body, it increased in diameter.

At several points, the creatures entered the spine of the individual, with several of them following a final channel through the C1 and C2 vertebrae into the skull. It is not possible to confidently identify the maximum number of creatures which this individual may have hosted, but a conservative minimum count is 12.

All the ribs, femurs, radius, humerus, and ulna showed considerable damage. Having examined the wear pattern caused by the invading species' teeth, it is my personal opinion the pain would have been excruciating for the individual concerned. No remains of the creatures were found within the skeletal material, or within the high organic content soils in the surrounding area.

[18] Fill [18] produced a large amount of human bone (205kg by weight). All types of human skeletal remains were represented, including femurs, ribs, vertebrae, skulls, and illium. All bones showed some form of damage from a bladed weapon. The evidence varied from precise butchery marks, particularly around the tendons of the long bones, to frenzied strikes. The cuts are consistent with the injuries seen on the skull in context [13], and it is my belief that the same blade was used.

In total, around 15 individuals were identified using the presence of diagnostic skull elements. Due to the fragmentary nature of the bones, this is a bare minimum, and the count could be much higher.

None of the skeletal remains from [18] show the same pattern of internal damage as the skull, phalanges and skeleton recovered elsewhere in Trench 3.

~

**Appendix Five**
**Specialist Ceramic Report by Diane Bansetten**
**The "Carrion Knoll Bowl"**

In many ways, the vessel is typical Samian ware displaying the characteristic high-quality burnished red slip. The bowl has a slightly deeper profile than usual (300m diameter x 200mm deep).

The main difference is in the decoration. While the scenes displayed on Samian vessels are hugely varied, depicting everything from hunting to pornography, I can think of no comparative to the designs on the Carrion Knoll Bowl.

The same panel repeats three times. Each shows a group of humanoid figures. I use the term humanoid advisedly. While they display the proportions typical of 2nd century AD figurative art, the humanoids are fringed with what I first took to be some kind of fur. On closer inspection and following consultation with a colleague (J. Sanders pers. comm.), they have more in common with certain types of coral.

It appears to represent a series of cylindrical polyps emerging from every inch of the skin. The segmented form is clearly defined and, using a hand lens, the fan of teeth can be seen at the terminus of each strand.

Only the humanoid faces are clear, which are rendered in such extreme and precise agony that this author assumes the potter drew something he witnessed first-hand.

I must also comment on the residual fragments of the bowl recovered from fill [10]. In nearly thirty years as a professional Romano-British ceramic specialist, I have never encountered bone and pottery fused together in such a way. During the firing process, the presence of an entire finger bone in the vessel wall would cause the bowl to explode. This would suggest that the finger bone has been introduced later. Yet once the bowl has been fired, any attempt to force the finger tip through the wall would cause considerable damage. The presence of the slip on the bone suggests that the pottery has melted somehow and then reset, trapping the fingers in the clay.

## Conclusion
Due to the unique and extremely disturbing nature of the decoration, the Carrion Knoll Bowl is unparalleled, certainly in British archaeology. The presence of the herbs surrounding the vessel, as well as the as yet unidentified contents, suggest that it had a very specific ritual purpose.

NB. A smear of the gel-like substance still adhered to the inside of the vessel when it arrived. During the unpacking this slid out and fell onto a pottery sherd from my reference collection. The glaze and decoration of this other fragment dissolved in front of my eyes. There may still be traces within the Carrion Knoll Bowl, and I would highly recommend that any further work is carried out following Hazmat guidelines.

**Further work**
In addition to regular consolidation and conservation work, I would recommend approaching a marine biologist to establish the identity of the coral deforming the humanoid figures in the decoration.

~

**Appendix Six**
**Organic material recovered from the Carrion Knoll Samian Bowl**
The material in the Samian bowl recovered from layer [11] was recognised in the cut of pit [05].

When the overlying archaeological material was excavated, the substance was visually inspected before removal by staff from Danburn Archaeological Conservation Laboratories.

The substance had the appearance and texture of aspic. Transparent and gelatinous, several inclusions were visible:

1. A fragment of skin and intact fingernail. The whole fingerprint was recognisable. Hopefully when the material is back in the lab, this can be recovered and examined further.

2. Several flower petals and mushrooms. Neither could be identified from a visual inspection and will require specialist study.

3. Clustered around the base appeared to be 20+ sinuous, segmented polyps, none more than 10mm long. Without cutting into the substance, it is difficult to determine whether they are organic or mineralised.

[Handwritten note]

(These observations of the Carrion Knoll Bowl's contents are from visual examination on site. The material was immediately shipped to the Danburn Archaeological Conservation Laboratory for analysis. In the last two weeks, there has been no further communication. At the time of publication, phone calls and emails have gone unanswered. If we have not received a response after the weekend, we will be in touch with emergency services to gain access.)

# Zaun König

Looking back, Skirethorpe Quarry was always going to be my last archaeology site. I'd been working the circuit for ten years, moving from job to job, and archaeology unit to archaeology unit. After a decade I'd had enough of working through the winter in chemsuits on building sites where we were seen as a problem, with short term contracts and shitty accommodation.

Don't let anyone tell you archaeology is romantic or glamorous because it's not. Fascinating, yes. Important? Absolutely. A stable career with long term prospects and job satisfaction. My knees and my bank account spent a decade disagreeing.

Skirethorpe did have some advantages. Multivallate Archaeology was a good unit, their project managers and project officers all experienced field archaeologists, and they were good at keeping their staff informed about the contract situation. The pay was good, and the accommodation? Some of the best accommodation I've had on an away site. Three holiday cottages next to each other. Own rooms, not having to share. Enough space in the communal areas for us all to socialise, but have privacy if we need to. Enough hot water to clean the site away at the end of the day. All would have been good, if it wasn't for the archaeology. And the weather.

It had rained solidly on site for six weeks and we'd found nothing interesting. Finding nothing is okay if the weather is lovely, and putting up with constant rain is bearable if you're working on interesting archaeology. Finding nothing and getting so soaked your clothes are covered in mildew wears down even the most experienced archaeologist after a month and a half. And with one look around the site hut you could tell. The morale was so low it was ground into the mud-covered floor every time someone walked in.

No-one spoke to each other, losing themselves in books and newspapers. Not because they had fallen out, but we were all old enough and experienced enough to know negativity was infectious, and we also knew we weren't going anywhere soon.

The quarry manager hated us. He hated what we did, he hated that he had to put up with our presence, he hated that we were holding up the next stage of quarrying (in his eyes). After six weeks on that godforsaken site I truly believe he hated us personally. I don't remember his name. Not that it matters anymore. We're past the point where names are important. All that mattered to him was, we were in the way, and we weren't finding anything. Still, the County Archaeologist wouldn't discharge the planning condition and improve everyone's winter. The geophysics and the trial trenching all suggested we should be swimming in iron age archaeology. Instead we were just swimming.

We weren't all cynical veteran diggers. Multivallate was good at taking on newly graduated archaeologists and sticking them on real sites with real archaeology (or not). They'd found jobs for five of them. Two left after the first week of rain, another after they were asked to do some surveying they believed was beneath them. (I thought Sophie was going to bury that one on site. Instead she drove him to the train station and told him to fuck off and not come back). The ones that stayed were good and diligent and willing to learn. Including Jack.

Jack listened. He didn't complain when the old hands lit their roll ups in the site hut as they poured over paperwork, or try to turn the radio off if the music was more than a decade old. He didn't try to start interesting moral debates. He sat in the site hut and kept to himself, went out to dig his trench and came back in. Repeat ad infinitum. Only if you watched him over time would you have seen his shoulders slump and all the enthusiasm leave him.

Sophie grabbed me as I was leaving to walk back onto site.

"You busy at the moment?" She paused and took a lungful of smoke, and I envied her the heat she would feel for a moment.

"Just finishing up another empty trench," I said. "Why? Do you have some internationally significant archaeology for me to wallow in?"

"I'm worried about him," she said, pointing after Jack with her roll up.

"Afraid he might find something interesting?"

"Fuck off," she said with no malice. We had known each other since we both started digging. Coming into each other's orbit over the years like half forgotten comets. "He's in an area where there was a geophysics anomaly, and he's also in an area that is constantly flooded."

"The whole site is constantly flooded," I said.

"I don't want him to miss anything," she continued. "He's good, but he's young."

"And not used to this sort of thing?"

Sophie nodded.

"His training dig was working on a multi year project excavating a viking burial mound."

"In summer?" I asked, already knowing the answer.

"In summer," Sophie said. Her roll up dropped to the floor and was already sodden before it hit the mud.

"Just so you know though, if we find anything, I'm taking all the credit," I said, smiling.

"I expect nothing less from a glory hunter like yourself."

I made a detour to the toolshed and grabbed myself a bucket, a sponge and a mutilated milk container – realistically the most useful tool on site – then walked between the other trenches to where Jack sat trying to trowel back the sodden clay.

It's hard to get across how wet a clay site can be in winter and how difficult it becomes to do the job. The problem with clay is, it's no better in summer, when the heat just cracks the soil and makes it almost impossible to see the features in the ground. I'm not sure which is worse.

The trench was a mess, churned up mud visible in the areas the water didn't cover, and the water covered most of it. Jack was fighting a losing battle with himself and the excavation.

"I've come to give you a hand," I said, stepping down beside him. I watched his shoulders slump a little more. Everyone wants to think they can do the job, and the thought that the boss has sent someone in to help, or worse to take over, can be corrosive. "What do you want me to do?"

The look of defeat was replaced by one of confusion. Why was I, a veteran of ten years who had spent every winter digging outside, got trench foot three times, frostbite once, and alcoholic poisoning more often than I cared to mention, asking him what he wanted me to do? He couldn't process it, but I can tell you now, here. Because it was his trench. I hadn't worked on it yet, and while I could guess what needed doing, to jump in and start ordering him about would probably finish any enthusiasm he had for the job.

"I'm trying to clean up, but I'm fighting a losing battle," he said. "Maybe help with that?"

I smiled, not that he could probably see it behind my coat, but I hope it came across in my voice.

"You carry on there, and I'll get rid of the flood down this end. Is that OK?"

He nodded, and I knelt down the far end, scooping out the worst of the water with the mutilated milk jug, then soaking up the last until the sponge was more mud than anything else.

"Is that OK?" I said standing back. He nodded, already seeing the job wasn't impossible and it wasn't going to defeat him.

"Would it be OK if I checked this corner," I said, pointing with my trowel. "And if it's clear, we can dig a sump. Everything seems to be running down that way."

He nodded again, and I got to work. By lunchtime the trench was looking clearer, and though not dry and not tidy, it was better.

I sat in the site hut, leaning forward on the table, and slowly stirred my tea until it was the colour of bricks, then dropped the teabag in the bin.

There was a bit of a hierarchy in the sitehut, though everyone was fairly laidback, with the older diggers like Big Bob Benton, who liked to sit at the top of the table, his sandwiches spread on Wednesday's Guardian as he searched the Heritage pages for jobs that just weren't there. Or Karen and Bill, the couple who met on a site, and spent all their time in a corner not speaking to each other, unless they were sent to different sites when they'd do nothing but talk *about* each other. Sophie sat at the top of the table. Not for a reason of superiority – in all my years digging I've not met anyone else less interested in lording it over people than Sophie – but because that's where all the paperwork was spread out. The site matrix, and the context sheets recording the archaeological features she spent most of her time checking. Then the others, the younger diggers inserted around the older lags. I noticed Jack sitting close, but not near enough to impose, and when I stood up to go to the door to have a smoke, he followed me.

"Thanks for this morning," he said. I offered him a roll up, but he shook his head.

"No worries," I said. "We should have it finished by this afternoon if we don't find anything."

That 'If' slowly evaporated throughout the day.

In commercial archaeology you are doing the job for someone else, and that means you have to prove you found nothing, if there's nothing to be found. That means cleaning back for photographs, even if there's nothing there to photograph. Even if it's been raining constantly for six weeks and the site's flooded. Even if your skin is starting to rot from your bones because you're damp all the time.

We were trowelling back the base of the trench when I spotted the pottery rim, black and flecked against the pale brown of the mud. I didn't say anything. I wanted to know if Jack would see it too when he looked back over the area he'd cleaned. He did. Just took him a bit longer.

"Something over here," he said, standing up and stretching out the cramps from his leg. "What do you reckon?"

"What do you reckon?" I said. He knelt down and teased away the dirt with his trowel, to get a better look at the fabric of the pottery.

"Quick guess, it's iron age, but I'm not sure about these small white stones to either side."

"Small white stones?" I said, kneeling down to have a closer look. "Fuck."

~

"Are you sure?" Sophie said as she walked alongside me from the sitehut back to the trench. The other diggers could tell something had been found. Something important. They could taste it on the air. On the rain.

"Of course I'm sure. I dug enough of them on that cemetery job in Hull."

We both worked on that excavation and didn't need to say anything else.

Reaching the trench I called Jack out and we stood on the side as Sophie jumped in to look for herself. Even over the sound of the wind I heard her swear.

"We have a licence in place?" I said.

"Yes, but the County Archaeologist said that they wanted to see any burials before we started lifting them, and the quarry manager is going to shit at this," she said, climbing back out. "Don't do anything here. Can you keep an eye on everyone while I set up a site meeting?"

I nodded and watched her walk back to the hut, swearing all the way.

The meeting took place in the rain. I sat in the site hut with Jack watching Sophie and the quarry manager crowd around the County Archaeologist, each trying to put forward their arguments.

"What do you think they're talking about?"

I looked up from my book. There was no paperwork from the trench to do yet. That would come later and in abundance.

"What do you mean?"

"Human remains. We have to lift them. Dignity of the dead and all that," Jack said, remembering a phrase he'd heard in a university lecture. "What's to discuss?"

I put my book to one side and took a sip of my tea.

"We will be lifting the skeleton. No question. The issue is, how many more are out there. Where there's one burial, normally there are more. The quarry manager will be arguing it's just an isolated stiff. County Mountie will want to open up the whole area to check for more graves. Sophie will be in the middle of them wanting to open the whole area, but knowing it will scare off the client, the quarry, so will argue for extending the trench and seeing what happens then."

"What do we do, until they finish deciding?"

I looked at him and smiled.

"We drink tea and look busy."

Half an hour later Sophie came back into the site hut, looked at me and Jack as if she wanted to say something, instead choosing to sit down and roll a cigarette.

"So, what's the plan?"

She said nothing for a moment, instead lighting the roll up and taking a huge lungful of smoke.

"Needed that," she said. "The plan is to just extend the trench to uncover the rest of the burial, lift it, then we will have another meeting. Because what I need on this site are more meetings."

"More meetings than archaeology," I said.

Sophie took another lungful of smoke and blew it toward the ceiling.

"Are you still here?"

~

I stood next to Jack by the trench, far enough back so we didn't collapse the edge, watching the 360° excavator rumble across the site. We carried on staring at the small white bones, just visible in the mud, while the machine driver changed his bucket for a toothless one, before jumping down and walking across.

"Now then, Jacob," I said, holding out my hand. The driver shook it and stepped back.

"Usual deal?" He said.

"Usual deal."

Like archaeologists, machine drivers often moved from contract to contract, and I'd worked on sites with Jacob twice before.

"You should get your ticket," he said, climbing back into his cab. "Lot less rain in here."

"Why bark yourself, when you can hire a dog to do it for you."

Jacob laughed, the joke mild compared to those he would probably hear later in his own site hut. In ten minutes he had the buckets switched, and in forty we had the extension to the trench pulled, the top soil and subsoil piled to one side.

"Do you want me to get a dumper down? Get that shifted?" he said.

I shook my head.

"Human remains. We need to go over that to make sure we don't miss anything."

"Anyone I know?" he asked.

"Not yet," I said, glancing at Jack, who was already climbing into the trench to start cleaning back.

Jacob laughed and walked back to his machine. Looking back on that joke from here, from now, it doesn't seem so funny.

We began to clean up the trench ready for excavation, trowelling back the sodden clay, though truth be told we carried as much out on our boots as in our buckets.

Jack was quiet, not like some diggers you work alongside who never shut up, but talkative enough we had some good conversations.

He found the limestone first, scraping his trowel along the off white stone and jarring his wrist.

"Is it natural?" he said, cradling his arm and trying to run life back into the joint.

"Looks like it," I said, but I was wrong. It wasn't natural, as solid as it was. Nothing in that trench was natural and everything that happened later, the unnatural, radiated from that single hole in the ground.

A definition might help here. When archaeologists talk about natural, what they usually mean is the lowest undisturbed geology or soil that the archaeology is cut into. In this case it made sense that the limestone would be the natural. It was what formed the geology beneath the site. The reason they were quarrying there. The reason we were there at all.

It was Jack who found the problem with the limestone too.

I was working at the far end, making sure the sump was keeping the trench clear of water. Jack was doing a good job of cleaning up the stone. Neither was particularly glamorous work, but clearing the water was cold and dirty, and I wanted him to keep his enthusiasm. Maybe that was a mistake too.

"What do you make of this?" he said, shouting to make himself heard over the wind that was turning the fine rain into needles. The idea archaeology stops when it's raining is another lie the TV told you.

"Limestone. Natural. I thought we'd got past that," I said, sheltering my eyes to look at him.

"Then why do the bones go underneath the limestone."

I knew he was wrong; it wasn't his fault. The conditions were more than shit, and trying to work out the stratigraphic relationship between anything was hard enough at the best of times, but there was no way the human skeleton was sealed into the ground by solid natural limestone. Except it was.

I jumped in and took over. Something I'd tried to avoid doing all the time we were working together, and I saw his face drop, but I'd had enough, and I was cold and tired, and sick of the site, and archaeology, and... well, you get the idea. So I told him to go and do some paperwork, and I knelt down where he'd been working, teasing away the topsoil to make things clearer, tidying up as I watched the rain rivulet down the fractured stone, and as I worked, delicate and fast at the same time, it became obvious he was right. Two femurs emerged from under the limestone, and what was even stranger – because it never rains, it pours – the bones were pinned to the ground by what looked like iron staples, the geology lapping over the metal.

"You're taking the piss," Sophie said as we walked across to the trench. Jack trailed after and you could feel the murmur running through the other diggers on site. We hadn't said anything, but they knew something strange had been found, or interesting, or just a distraction, and soon we had a parade of mildewed archaeologists walking across to the trench, hanging back slightly so it didn't seem like they were really having a break.

Once she was happy we weren't taking the piss, Sophie walked off a little distance to swear and smoke, while Jack and I stood around looking lost.

I'd dug enough sites to have confidence, but archaeology is a job of the unexpected and this was off the scale.

Sophie came back and pointed to the bones in the mud.

"It has to be dumped on top. It has to be. I want you to work around it. Get the machine in to extend either side and see what is going on. How far this stone dump goes, clean it, record it, and then lift it to get that skeleton done."

"It looks like natural," I said quietly, realising straight away it was a mistake to say anything.

"It can't be fucking natural, can it. Probably some kind of concrete. Maybe Roman. Get it dealt with, and if you don't think you can, I'll put someone else in the trench."

I looked around the other old lags on the site. I'm not saying I was the most easygoing person, but I was pretty laidback, and I'm not sure Jack would have lasted the morning alone with someone like Big Bob who liked to talk about either politics or his sexual conquests, both largely fictitious, or JoJoJo who took pride in not washing his clothes from the start of a site until the end. I was no saint, but for Jack I was best of a bad bunch.

Jack watched as I called Jacob back with the machine, and we both watched him extend the trench, following the top of the limestone, until it sloped down too deep. There was no question it was natural and there was no question the skeleton was trapped. The only question was what we did about it.

By the time Jacob was finished, it was afternoon tea break, and I took the opportunity to chat to some of the other diggers. Ask if they had dug anything similar on other sites. Archaeology is a hivemind of fractured knowledge, and the best sites work when you pool that information. The only time anyone had seen a similar situation was a huge dump of compacted building rubble over an iron age hut circle, that looked like natural stone until they found the brick fragments in it. There were no brick fragments this time.

I didn't see Jack all tea break. When I finished chatting and drinking, I headed back to where we were working, our little corner of that damp kingdom, and found him kneeling in front of the skeleton, trowel in one hand, the other tightly closed into a fist.

"Do you know what these are?" he said, and opened his fingers.

The bones were delicate and fragile, hollow and easily broken, but Jack had been careful. They were a tiny bird skeleton, and now I looked where he was working, I could see the mud was full of them.

"It's a wren," he said. "The Germans call it Zaunkönig. The Fence King. Lord of Barriers. We've broken the barrier. We shouldn't have broken the barrier."

I think it was something in the bones. Maybe the stone, but not the water. I don't think it was in the water, because I was okay and I was steeped in the stuff. Soaked with it. But Jack. Something changed that day.

Thursday was our Friday night. Most people headed back home on a Friday, so if we would all go to the pub on a Thursday and go for a drink (most of us used to head to the pub every night, but Thursdays we were all out).

Our local on that job was the Three Crowns, or the Three Dead Kings as it was known locally. I was stood by the bar watching a pint of Guinness settle when I noticed Sophie slide in next to me.

"Don't forget you need to carry on sorting out that trench tomorrow," she said, waiting until the barman caught her eye before turning to look at me properly.

"Have you ever known me to get so wrecked I couldn't work properly?"

"Northampton?"

I sighed and took a sip of the stout the barman had just handed me.

"Northampton was my last night, and I still turned up on site in the morning. After two hours sleep."

"You were still drunk."

"Still worked though."

She shook her head, ordered a beer and leaned forward on the bar, head in her hands.

"Can you go over and check on Jack?"

"Do I have to be his babysitter outside work too? He's a nice kid, but I want my own time."

She shook her head.

"Of course not, but something isn't right. He's been sat by himself all night, and every time anyone goes to talk to him he just stares at them until they go away." She paused. I took another sip of the Guinness. It tasted good. It felt good, in the way that only beer can after a long day in the rain.

"You didn't pick on him, did you?" she asked. I tried not to look offended. Sophie knew how I felt about onsite bullying. She'd seen me deal with a couple over the years.

"I'll ignore that," I said. "But I will go and talk to him."

She didn't smile, or thank me. Instead, she just stood at the bar, sipping her drink, and for the first time I really saw what that site was doing to her, and I wondered if she would still be in archaeology when we finished.

I took my drink over to where Jack sat alone. I couldn't quite work that out. We might have been a bunch of rugged individualists, but we were fairly sociable, and the pub wasn't big enough to really pick and choose. Still, everyone was crowded into the far end of the pub, and Jack was sat at a table by himself, an untouched pint in front of him. It was only when I pulled up the stool opposite that I noticed the bones on the table. Small and hollow and fragile. My hackles went up straight away.

"Those better not be what I think they are?"

"Wren bones. They're very delicate."

Now I was closer, I could see they were cleaner than the ones under the hands of the burial, with meat still attached.

"I found them outside," he continued. "Delicate aren't they?"

He reached out and passed me one. There was a lightness to it, and despite myself I squirmed and put it back on the table. The backs of his hands were cut. Not hidden like most self harming, but that didn't mean it could be dismissed. Maybe he had made them obvious to make the conversation easier.

"Catch yourself on the limestone?" I said, giving him an out if he needed it. He looked down as if realising he still had hands.

"These? No, I did them myself. Flint. Nothing else is quite sharp enough. I need to cut in

- 164 -

pockets, but even with a sharp blade it hurts, so I'm taking it slow."

He reached in his pocket and brought out a flint blade, the edge rippled from the workmanship needed to make it so sharp.

"Is that from another site?" I said.

"I made it myself. Never done it before, but I knew how to. Just knew how to."

I was going to ask where he found flint in an area that was so heavy in limestone, but while I was thinking what to say, he picked up the blade and slid it into one of the wounds, the blade scraping on the tendons.

"I have to do it slow," he said. "It hurts so much. But I need to do it, to fit the bones back inside."

Look, this was a different time, before everyone was aware of self harm, but even then if he was a friend, a close friend, I might have said something. Tried to get him to stop. I was tired and my clothes smelt of damp, and I had stuff going on elsewhere off site that I was trying to ignore, so ignoring another thing was easy. There were a lot of people attracted to archaeology because they had problems they didn't need to face head on. Jack might have been a bit young to be going that way, but he was no different to any of us. At least he didn't seem to be after I'd had four Guinnesses and a few whiskeys. I don't think an intervention would have changed anything at that time. Instead, I walked away and joined the conversation on the other table, leaving him to his flints and his bird bones.

~

I wasn't going home back then. The accommo was booked out over the weekends too, and it was more comfortable than the place I had waiting for me. Instead, I spent most of my time reading, or watching DVDs on the site computer. Most other people had families or partners to go back to. Occasionally someone else stayed, but not often.

I didn't even know Jack had not gone home, until the quarry manager turned up hammering on the door.

I looked at my watch. It was ten am on Sunday morning, and while I got dressed the hammering continued, until I opened the door.

"Was it you?" he said, before I had chance to speak.

"Was it me, what?"

"Was it you who was up on site? Someone was poking around that trench yesterday. Caught them on the CCTV. It was you or that rat faced little shit you were working with."

I guessed he was talking about Jack, but as far as I knew then, Jack had gone home.

"Look," I said, trying to sound as reasonable as I could. "It's not unusual for sites to attract nighthawks going in after work to try and find artefacts they can sell. Your PR put out a press release last week to the local newspapers. Probably caught someone's eye. Don't know why, though. We've found fuck all worth nicking."

"If that's the case, why were they wearing a hi-vis with your company's logo emblazoned across the back?"

I saw there was no way to calm him, but I did the best I could.

"Leave it with me, and I'll try and find out what's going on. Might be someone left some personal kit on site and thought they could get it without anyone noticing."

"Like fuck I'm going to leave it to you," he said, walking away. He stopped halfway across the carpark. "I'm ringing your senior manager tomorrow, and the County Archaeologist, and I'll have you shower of dickheads thrown off so we can get on and do some proper fucking work."

I closed the door, rubbed my head and walked through to the kitchen, trying to decide what to do next. Whether to bother Sophie on a Sunday morning, or let everything play out without my interference. Without having to ruin Sophie's weekend. I poured myself a coffee and walked over to the french doors that looked out on the shared patio, deciding to let nature take its course.

Jack had moved all the plastic chairs to one side, and was sitting in the middle of the garden, stripped to the waist. His chest was smeared with dirt, his arms covered in scabs and streaks of blood.

You think you know what you'll do in these types of situations. Ring an ambulance, or even just shout "What the fuck do you think you're doing?" I'm sure the quarry manager would have, seeing Jack out there in the middle of winter half naked and covered in shallow cuts. I was never so decisive, and by the time I was arriving at a course of action – I'm talking thirty seconds, not like it was an hour of sitting there watching him – the water had started.

First, it came from the wounds, seeping out, like rain around a badly fitted window frame, then slowly the pressure increased, edges of his skin bulging where it pressed out from between his severed muscles. The liquid dripped onto the floor, rivulets forming on the paving slabs until it seeped into the gaps between. Watching, I thought how much Jack's wounds were like the spaces between the slabs. Then he turned to me, opened his eyes, his mouth widening as if he was about to speak, and a torrent erupted from his face, cascading down his front.

That seemed to wake me up. I searched for the patio door key, wrenched them open, and stepped outside. He was gone. I don't know how he moved so quickly, but he was no longer there, and where he had been sitting, there was little more than a damp patch on the concrete.

I stood looking around the patio and the garden. There was nowhere he could have gone. The doors to all the other cottages were shut and locked. I tried them one by one, and I didn't see him again until the start of work on Monday morning.

~

When Sophie drove down the lane to pick us up, there wasn't an opportunity to talk to her. The minibus was already full of other diggers, and even though I tried to say something about needing to speak to her later, she closed me down.

"We're running late, and Jack isn't here. Can you go and get him?"

I nearly used that as an opportunity to say something, but Jack emerged from his accommo, short sleeves on despite the cold, his skin clear of wounds and blood.

By the time we reached site, the office had tried to ring Sophie on the work mobile five times, and when we arrived at the quarry, she stayed in the van to take the call.

She wasn't speaking to them for long, and as she climbed down, I took the chance to talk.

"I need to discuss something with you," I said. She rolled her eyes.

"I know. The quarry manager was a prick. Came out and gave you shit on your day off. I will have a word, but I can understand why he was pissed off."

"Maybe someone forgot something and came back to work to pick it up," I said. "But I think it was more likely to be nighthawks."

"I agree," Sophie said, rolling herself a cigarette. "It looks like the toolstore was left open. Not much worth stealing, but it makes sense that they might grab some hi-vis."

She took a lungful of smoke, looked at the ground, then directly at me.

"I'm going to be absolutely straight with you, because we've known each other a long time. With someone creeping around the site, I need some good news to get the quarry manager off our back. He's a prick, but he's a prick that can cause problems. Is there any chance you and Jack can get the stone lifted from off the body so we can at least look like we're making progress?"

"That's what I wanted to talk to you about. Jack. I'm a bit worried about him," I said.

She looked at me and smiled, then nodded behind me.

"I know it's weird seeing him so chatty, but I think actually finding something has given him back some enthusiasm. Or maybe your positive go getting attitude is rubbing off on him."

I followed where she was looking. Jack had already got his tools and was walking across to the trench saying hello to everybody, whether they were in any mood to respond or not.

"Seeing anyone cheerful in this shithole is unnerving," she said. "But you do have the only decent archaeology on the site."

The rain had let up for once, and by the time I reached the trench, he'd already sponged out the water, sleeves rolled up. I looked without looking, but there were no scars or wounds on his arms, and when he spoke he sounded normal, even a little bit more positive than before.

With all the photographs and records done for the limestone, we began to remove it. This was brutal but careful work. We needed to find faults in the stone to split it, but make sure as we got lower down the body below wasn't damaged. We soon had the bulk removed, and Jack worked at handing me the pieces as I barrowed them away. Finally, just before afternoon tea break, we had the full burial revealed.

There was nothing unusual about the skeleton itself, apart from the position of the arms, which seemed to have been stretched over its head, the metal staples holding them in place, echoing those around the legs we'd already seen. What was unusual was the material on top of the burial.

At first it was difficult to make out, and my first idea was that it was from old roots. Minerals sometimes form along them, so it's not unusual to see weird metallic shapes in the soil, but these were far too regular.

Jack stood beside me as I looked down into the trench.

"You know what that is?" he said.

"I'm not sure," I said. When he next spoke, everything else faded away. The smell of diesel from the quarry machines, the sound of conversation, even the distant sound of the motorway. There was just me listening and Jack talking.

"It's a fence. Fence for the Fence King. All the boundaries are coming down." Then the world shuddered and everything came rushing back, and I realised that the quarry face had been blasted, sending shockwaves through the ground. We were far enough away, but still the sensation rippled through my bones as I tried to concentrate on Jack's expression. The grin. The grin would stay with me for a very long time.

Of course, I got Sophie to find out what she wanted us to do. She seemed happier now the limestone was gone, and she had convinced herself it was some kind of later dump. A weird burial was easy to deal with. A weird burial underneath geology was another level entirely.

We took some quick photographs and cleared up our tools, climbing into the van for the ride back into the accommodation, to get washed up and have some food. Some of the others were heading down to the pub, but my enthusiasm had gone, so I made my apologies and went back to my room. I was the only one left in our holiday cottage. Instead of sitting in the shared area, I laid on my bed reading a book, the radio playing quietly in the background.

I noticed the smell first, the same stench of mud and dirt from the trench, slightly sweet and cloying. I looked up from my book and saw Jack stood there, his arms hanging in front of him, fingers laced together.

Although we had to share space, the different cottages had different keys, and one of the others must have left the door open.

"How did you get in," I said, sitting up as he continued to stare at me.

"I told you, the barriers are coming down. The boundaries are suppurating. The Zaun König is almost free, and everything will tumble. The divisions between worlds, between people. One flesh will be all flesh. One wound will be all wounds. We will all be entwined."

I'm not a small person, and many years of mattocking on site meant I had the strength to back it up if I needed to. I swung my legs around and stood up from the bed.

"I think you best fuck off back to the other cottage," I said. "And hope I don't mention this to the office."

Let me be straight. Archaeology attracts a lot of people who wouldn't fit in elsewhere. People with substance problems. People with undiagnosed mental health problems. People who didn't play well with others. Maybe it was the short term contracts that meant you could move from one company to another. I'm saying this to explain why I didn't do anything. Jack wasn't a threat to me. I once shared a house with a guy who would draw devices from the Key of Solomon on the front room floor to protect us from the spirits that might be released while we were cooking pasta. Weird people were never an issue.

Looking back, Jack should have set off alarm bells. At the time, I just decided to leave him alone out of work and keep to myself.

After he left, and I don't exactly remember him leaving, I found the bones on the carpet by my bed. Although I'd done an archaeozoology module at uni I couldn't have told you what they were for sure, but I knew, and when I showed them to Marianne, our bones expert, when she came out to site the next day, I already knew.

"They look like wren bones. Tiny aren't they?" she said, cradling them in her hands like the bird was still alive. "Pretty complete too. They're so small they often get lost or damaged. Did these come off site?"

I shook my head.

"Found them in the garden at the accommo," I said.

"Probably a cat got bored with its kill. Nice find though."

"Take it," I said. I can't explain why but it felt right for Marianne to have it, and truth be told there was something wrong about that bird. I'm not squeamish. I worked on the big London cemetery, all those 18th and 19th century bodies far more preserved than they should have been. Some never worked again after that site. The intact bodies were bad enough. The human soup, people liquefied by time, and the smell in those vaults? That stays with you. I'm used to death, but that bird was not right and I couldn't tell you why to this day.

~

We were just cleaning up the mineralised wood when Sophie walked over to the edge of the trench. I glanced up, shielding my eyes against the rain.

"Jack, you need to come with me," she said. There was no doubt or argument in her voice. No space for debate. She was angry. Very fucking angry. "You best come along too."

I followed behind them, walking toward the sitehut. We went in. There was only the three of us in there. The gas heater was on and the room was too hot, the air thick with over-stewed tea and sodden waterproofs drying on the backs of chairs.

"We've been noticing some vandalism," Sophie said, rolling herself a cigarette. "Records changed, the site matrix altered." She paused looking up at Jack. "Some finds going missing."

I didn't say anything. I didn't speak. I wasn't sure if I was there as a witness or an advocate. In the meantime I was furniture and tried not to get involved.

"We searched your room, Jack. We found the finds in your bag." She dropped a small plastic bag on the table, the writing on the white plastic strip smudged, but the site code still visible. "I don't want explanations or excuses. I want you off my site now."

Jack's face broke into the widest smile, and for a moment I could see far too many teeth.

What he did next was never forgotten by any digger who saw it.

People think that because we remove the past from the ground, and when we're working on commercial sites we can remove it fast at times, that we're reckless with it. That we don't care. Nothing could be further from the truth. We're not heroes, but sometimes we're the only ones who will see that post medieval pottery no-one else would care about, or the only people who will pause a cable-laying company to quickly record a stone floor barely visible in a narrow trench. We care about the archaeology more than anything. That's why what Jack did next was talked about on excavations around the country for months.

Leaving the sitehut, he didn't bother to pick up any of his personal possessions. Instead he walked over to the trench. I followed him unsure what to do. What he was going to do. By the time I got there, he was kneeling down beside the skeleton. I couldn't reach him in time to stop him.

Reaching over, he hooked his fingers beneath the mineralised wood, and with one movement wrenched it free, scattering the artefact onto the spoil heap. Slowly he stood, and walked over to me, leant in close and whispered.

"The fence is down. The Zaun König is free. The boundaries will congeal and collapse under their own weight, and then the Fence King will return and he will stitch us all together until there is no boundary between flesh and soil and wood and decay."

I know what I saw next. The other diggers on site say that Jack walked off, down the access road and left the quarry, laughing to himself, but I didn't see that, and I don't know how they did. What I saw is this.

Jack walked to the foot of the skeleton, and let himself fall onto the bones. As I watched his skin split, as if there was no longer enough to cover his muscles. I tried to move but I couldn't. I tried to turn away, but I couldn't. I could hear the meat of him seeping into the dirt, mixing with the mud and the grit and the bones already there. I don't know how long I watched, and I don't know how long it lasted, but when it finished, lying on the burial that still needed to be excavated, was a single dead wren, fifteen thorns pressed through its tiny chest pinning the feathers in place.

I did not pick it up, but that was not the last time I found one. When I got back to the accommodation, and finally went to bed, there was another wren on my pillow, the thorns fastening the bird to the cotton. I moved it, then slept on the floor.

There have been more, and they're increasing, and I know, I know, because I know about finds and offerings and I know that they are symbols from Jack, from the Zaun König. I know they are his messengers, his messages, and I know that Jack was right, and the boundaries are starting to fall.

I first wanted to be an archaeologist at seven years old, and many people are responsible for me achieving that ambition.

A huge thank you to the staff and students of the HND in Practical Archaeology, especially Tim and Stu, and the greatly missed Bill Putnam who first set up the course that so many of us benefited from.

Thanks to the diggers at the '94 Rectory Farm excavation, my first introduction to fieldwork. It was a baptism of fire and you were all so supportive.

I owe a huge debt to Professor Mark Edmonds who ran the MA in Landscape Archaeology when I was at Sheffield. You gave me space to explore my ideas about embodiment and hillforts, which completely changed the way I think about place, in turn influencing my fiction. Also, a shout out to my colleagues on the course. You made the MA one of the most enjoyable years of my life.

To all the archaeologists I've worked with over the years. Whether it's digging in a tiny trench in a bookshop basement, or excavating Roman graves surrounded by unexploded ordnance and contaminated soils, you approach the job with commitment, passion, humour, and dedication.

To John Buglass. It was a pleasure working with you over the years (and sorry about the finger...)

To Annie, as always I owe you the biggest debt. You've been there all the way through my career, whether I was working away for months on end, or arriving home reeking of riverine silts. I love you.

And finally to Charlie. If I do nothing else, I hope I can inspire you to find a career you love. You make me proud every day.

## Also by Steve Toase:

**Collections**
*To Drown in Dark Water* (Undertow Publications, 2021)

*Visit Steve Toase at his website:*
**stevetoase.wordpress.com**

*Now available and forthcoming from*
*Black Shuck Shadows:*

### Now available and forthcoming from Black Shuck Shadows:

*Now available and forthcoming from*
*Black Shuck Shadows:*

*Shadows 37 – Dirt Upon My Skin*

by Steve Toase

**blackshuckbooks.co.uk/shadows**